Rising from the Ashes

Anne K. Nagel

Nagela Press

Anchorage

Rising from the Ashes

This is a work of fiction. Characters and events portrayed in this book are fictional. Any resemblance to real people or events is purely coincidental.

Library of Congress Control Number: 2021904946

ISBN 978-0-9889676-5-6

Published in the United States by Nagela Press,
PO Box 210036, Anchorage, Alaska 99521-0036

Cover Design: SelfPubBookCovers.com/ElleArden

This book is dedicated to those who strive to envision, build and protect a better world.

A grateful tip of the pen goes to Beth and Justin.

Contents

Into the Unknown

Recruits were huffing and puffing. Special Forces training was difficult as it was, but it had recently gotten much more intense. The aliens had made increasing incursions into various areas of the world. With bombings from the alien ships in space becoming more frequent, the atmosphere had already become hazy. The particulates blocked the sun's rays and were starting to drive temperatures lower. At this early stage, it was a welcome respite from rampant worldwide warming, but the trend was disturbing.

Two soldiers watched the new recruits. The scene brought to mind their days in Green Beret training. That was a while ago, though. Now one was a sergeant and the other was a master sergeant.

"Jorland, Johnson, come with me." A seasoned superior officer motioned to them to follow. He led them to the general's headquarters and had them sit in an outer office. "Wait here till you're called." The older man turned and rapped on the door to the inner office. Once he disappeared inside, the two younger men turned questioningly to each other.

"Jason, did you do something?" Saul Johnson looked worried. "I'm more likely to be called in for a reprimand than you, but I haven't done anything – recently." Saul was the more "fly by the seat of his pants" guy. The infractions usually only merited minor rebukes, though. The means could be overlooked, as long as the outcome was successful.

"Not that I'm aware of, at least not this time," the confident Jason Jorland replied with a smile.

Jason, the dark-haired one, was thoughtful and detailed in his approach to a problem. That had earned him his master sergeant's rank. Saul was fair-haired and more outgoing. He was quick to think outside the box, though his carefree ways sometimes didn't set well with his superiors. The two couldn't have been more different than night and day. Yet with their abilities paired together, they made a formidable team. Both were still young enough to retain some brashness, though some of that had been seasoned with experience.

The general's aide opened the door to the inner office and called to the two waiting uncomfortably in the outer area. "Come in now," he said with no explanation.

The two walked briskly inside. They stood before the general and saluted him. The general saluted back and said, "Master Sergeant, Sergeant, have a seat." They both sat, nearly simultaneously, with military precision. They looked around at others seated with them, all attentive and apprehensive of what was going on.

Without even looking up from the papers he was checking, the general began to speak to the soldiers. "I'm sure you all have heard a lot of rumors, and there are a few incidents reported in the news that we couldn't keep quiet."

The grizzled high-ranking official grabbed a remote and flipped the TV on for the young soldiers to watch. "Here is some of the latest video retrieved from a recent encounter with the aliens. You can see one of their vehicles, dubbed 'walkers' by those who have already encountered them." The display showed a horrendous scene of a walker plowing through throngs of panicking civilians who were trying to run away. "We captured an alien coming out of one of these walkers. This tells us that they are alien-piloted vehicles, not drones or AI driven. We are beginning to understand their language. We now know they call themselves Xanites. Obviously, they can breathe our air. At this point, it is unknown if we have to deal with any xenobiological problems of contagion. We're only just learning what their capabilities and vulnerabilities are."

The general showed a video of a skinny, tall alien coming out of one walker. The armor he, she, or it wore didn't look airtight. Further video showed a creature that would almost look more at home in a deep-sea film.

The general flipped through other videos. “We all know that the situation is bad. The truth is, it’s worse than most people realize. We expect that things will continue to deteriorate because the Xanites have some advanced weaponry, though how superior it is to our own is yet to be determined. That fact has been obvious from the start. It is surmised that, given time, we could catch up. The question is: will we have the time to develop weaponry and armor advanced enough to counter theirs?”

The general paused to let that sink in. “They’ve put forces on the ground in various places and they have orbital firepower. They’ve taken out most of our satellites and made it increasingly difficult to replace those we’ve lost. We and our allies have had many of our military installations demolished. Even our space arm has its hands tied because of the GPS and communications blackout. Some intrepid pilots have tried going up pretty much blind and fighting by the seat of their pants. It was a heroic sacrifice. They were able to buy us a little more time.”

The two young men looked at each other, then to the others listening to this dire news. They turned back to the general, who spoke. “Without communications, our drones won’t work and we’re basically fighting with little intel and no coordination.”

Switching the video, the general paused in his address to watch scenes from around the world. They were all the same. People ran from cities through streets clogged with abandoned cars. Skyscrapers crumbled from aerial attacks. Mayhem and panic were rampant everywhere.

“There’s a lot of information we need to fight them successfully. It’s increasingly impossible to get useful intelligence from other nations. They’re just trying to survive, like we are. Each nation has been forced to proceed on its own in this. The president has decided that we are going to have to plan to fight an asymmetric war. The Green Berets excel at that. That is why I propose to transfer this group to a classified outfit. It isn’t being advertised because we don’t want information leaked to the Xanites. We also don't want the civilian population to panic. Otherwise, they are worse than useless – they're in the way. You're being sent to do what you know how to do – organize the population and create a resistance."

The general took a moment to reflect and looked at the soldiers seated before him. "This is perhaps the most important, and desperate, mission you all will ever be given. You have trained for this. We have to expect that this will be a long-term proposition. Along with organizing a resistance, you and others who will join this mission have got to see to it that government and society survive. Housing and mobile food kitchens are a start, to assist refugees and create safe areas to rebuild. The problem is, while you will be given supplies to last for a while, if this is a drawn-out conflict, you'll have to scavenge for resources and make your own weapons. This could wind up being a multigenerational mission."

The general showed more videos of throngs of people fleeing the now-devastated cities. "We have to anticipate there will be technological backslide. You'll need to train the younger generation; not only how to fight this enemy, but also how to bootstrap themselves back up. They'll have to recreate society and learn to govern themselves once again."

The general continued. "In this operation, groups of you will spread out and bring various areas under protection from attack. To do this, the populace would need to be organized to fight off the invaders. Once that is accomplished, the next stage would be to reestablish contact between some of these separate areas. They would be formed into city groups first. After that, bigger organizations would be created, growing from counties into states. The long-term goal would be unified government over all these areas. The result may not be the United States as it used to be, but the goal is to achieve unification once again."

The grim look in the general's eyes told the men more than their superior was saying. "You'll be expected to make reports as you can, and, for as long as we can, we'll respond. We expect there will come a point where we won't be able to assist you. Anticipate that. For the most part, you'll be on your own. You'll need to find and coordinate with others nearby. You're used to that. I can only hope that you can somehow eke out a life for yourselves in all this destruction."

***

"So, it looks like we're going to be sent to the Midwest," Saul said with his usual cheer once they'd gotten their assignment.

"Yeah. Don't remind me. Frigid winters and hot summers. Why couldn't they have sent some Alaskans to deal with the snow?" Obviously, Jason was less than enthusiastic about their posting.

The two met for coffee before heading out to their designated area. With their different approaches to a problem, they were sure to excel.

"Well, think about it this way. If they sent the Alaskans to the Midwest, they'd wind up sending us up there. More sun in the summer, true, but also more snow and longer winters than the Midwest. I'll take the shorter winters." Saul received the stink eye for that good-humored comment.

"Just wait till you see all the lake effect ice they can get." Jason gulped the last of his coffee and they stood to leave.

"Right, but the walkers will probably have a problem with the ice and snow – they aren't going to be as sure-footed as our treaded vehicles are." Saul followed his friend as they moved out of the coffee shop and headed off to their plane.

***

"This isn't as big or prepared a group as we were led to believe," Jason said quietly once they had seen what their task entailed.

"Yes, we've got a lot of work to do. They definitely need us," Saul agreed.

The two got busy determining the abilities of each of the refugees. The civilians were put to work at specific chores around the camp. The two soldiers utilized people with building experience. They raided home-improvement stores for lumber and building supplies. Soon, the work group had to scavenge abandoned buildings and go further afield to get more supplies when the local areas were picked clean of anything usable.

Multiple reports to headquarters showed the place was looking more like a settlement and less like a temporary encampment.

"Now that we've got various makeshift buildings in the process of being built, we can start to scrounge for medical supplies for a triage area and find people with medical training. We've put together some outdoorsmen who have weapons and hunting experience to find game to feed all the people coming into the settlement. We've scavenged from local grocery stores, but they've mostly been emptied. Word is getting out and people are trickling in. They all need food and safety. It gives us more people to mobilize, but it means we need more buildings to house them and a place to feed them."

The next report they sent showed more progress. "We still need medical personnel, but we've been able to put together a few mechanically-inclined people to repair any vehicles that might still run. We even took a few tracked vehicles from a dealership. Those snowmobiles will come in handy. Gas is in short supply, though."

The report suddenly got choppy when the screeching of metal on metal sounded nearby. "We're under attack. We've got walkers incoming!" The video went askew and the two soldiers hurried to get the able-bodied people who could fight up front. Those with guns and remaining ammunition took aim.

The video faded out. Obviously much later, the two soldiers continued their interrupted report. "We have to secure the area. There are a few trucks that can still run, so we're taking useless hulks that have been scavenged for parts and placing them around the perimeter for protection. We'll also have to set up some sort of watch, in case the walkers try to sneak back."

One afternoon, a woman strode fearlessly into the settlement. She was dirty and thin, but still pretty. Her dark hair was pulled into a messy ponytail. It was obvious she had been through a lot. Despite that, she still had an air of authority about her.

"I want to know who's in charge here," she told the first person that approached her. He didn't know what to do, so he just took her immediately to Jason and Saul.

Jason was the first to see her. He didn't speak, even after being told the woman was looking for someone in charge. It took a second before he got his wits about him again. "Can I help you? I'm Jason Jorland, by the way. Saul Johnson and I are here assisting these people to rebuild and protect themselves."

"This is quite the complex you've got here – at least, by present standards. What is this place, anyway?"

Jason latched on to that question to keep his mind in check. "We haven't bothered naming it yet. This isn't much right now, but it's going to be a town. Hopefully, it'll become a refuge for people from the nearby bombed-out areas to provide protection from the Xanites. We're planning a perimeter to protect the inhabitants. Now, what we need are tradespeople and medical personnel."

"Really." The woman smiled and Jason couldn't help enjoying that brief bit of sunshine in his cheerless existence. "I just so happen to know an EMT, if you could use one."

Saul walked in at that moment and broke Jason's concentration on the woman. Jason looked at him and said, "Good. You're here. This woman says she knows someone with medical skills." Turning back to the newcomer, he said, "By the way, I didn't catch your name."

"Well, I hadn't given it. First, why are you two doing this? What's in it for you? These days, everybody is in it for themselves."

"Our job is to help people form a resistance, simple as that." Jason wasn't sure why this stranger was putting up such opposition to telling them anything, so he tried a different approach. "How about we start with introductions? As I said, I'm Jason, and this is Saul. What may I call you?"

At that, the stranger laughed, breaking the tension that had begun to build. "I'm just not as sociable as I used to be, times being what they are. I'm Valerie, and in case you were wondering, I am the EMT."

Saul stepped over to shake her hand. "Good! We need medical help like crazy! We've scavenged a few things, but you could take a look and tell us what else might be good to have. Come with me – er – us, and we'll show you the future medical center." He looked at Jason, who followed along, frowning at Saul. Forgetting his senior officer was a breach of etiquette.

The three stepped outside the office tent and walked over to what would be the health building. "As you can see, it's still being built," the talkative Saul informed her.

The unfamiliar woman was given a summary of what supplies they had. She was able to provide a few ideas for additional materials to get. The two men proudly discussed the other buildings and how they would eventually be used. She listened quietly and intently. Then, she stepped over to the muddy road, in view of the forest beyond the buildings, and gave a piercing whistle. Out of the woods, a blonde woman came running.

"This is Ariella," Valerie said as the blonde woman came up to them, with a bow in hand and an improvised quiver of arrows at her back. "I'm expecting that you all are worthy of our help and trust," Valerie said with serious intent.

This time, it was Saul's turn to quietly stare at their visitor. Ariella was friendlier than her cohort. She stuck her hand out to shake Jason's, then turned to shake Saul's. When she did that, they both got caught up in gazing at each other. Jason gave a wry smile, since he'd been the same way with Valerie.

"Now that we're all introduced, Valerie has told us she's got medical expertise. What can you do, Ariella?" Jason got down to business.

Ariella bristled a bit at his brusque words. "Well, we disabled a couple walkers a few days ago. That's what I can do – what we both can do."

Jason was interested. "I'd like to hear how you did that."

"With these." The blonde woman reached into her quiver to pull out some straight sticks that were wider than arrows. They'd been whittled to a point on one end with a notch on the opposite end. "These sticks are made of hardwood. They can fly a short distance, though they aren't as good as arrows for most things. But lob them or jam them into a walker's leg joint and it won't walk too well. Keep doing it to the rest of its joints, and the machine will be completely crippled. You have to remember to keep moving after you shoot, though. When they fire back, they pack a punch."

Both Jason and Saul looked at each other, impressed. This was a maneuver that obviously worked. They could use it to fight back.

"We haven't tried bows and arrows. We used improvised explosives and hand grenades, but ran out of those early on. Your information verifies our findings that the legs are a major weak point. The rest of the walker seems to be more heavily armored, though," Saul said. He wasn't one to distain unorthodox tactics, as long as they were successful. "Do you think you could teach others to fashion sticks into weapons like these, and show them how to use them?"

Ariella thought briefly. "As long as they can use a bow, these will be straightforward to fire. If someone needs to be taught to make and use a bow, that'll take a little longer, but I can do it," she added with confidence. "The problem with these is their lack of range. People will need to be fairly close to get any accuracy."

Saul warmed to the problem and started thinking of solutions. "What could give you more power so you could stay back further?"

The blonde woman smiled and said, "Well, crossbows have more power than a bow, but a stick as thick as this wouldn't fit. Crossbows also take longer to reload."

"Crossbows, you say? I can see if some of the hunters have those. They might not work for this, but other uses present themselves. With ammunition becoming scarce, something that will give us meaningful striking power makes a good alternative. I think a mission to a sporting goods store might be in order!" Saul's mind was already at work.

Ariella and Valerie went with the raiding party. In the sporting goods section of a nearby store, they scavenged any available ammunition and crossbows and bolts. They also wanted to find any remaining medical supplies wherever they could scrounge them.

Since Ariella knew about the requirements of her bow, she let the crossbow users choose their favored bolts. She carefully considered the arrows she could use. "Most arrows are either aluminum or carbon fiber. The aluminum ones won't last as long, but either will do for light game. Neither are useful for crippling a walker," she reminded the others. "Even your bolts are often made of hardwood and are too slim to do much to a walker joint. The aluminum or carbon fiber ones, as well, would just be bent or crushed."

They heeded her words. Next, Saul had the party stop into the hardware section of the store to scout out the wooden dowels. "Would any of these be strong enough?"

She stopped to look closely at all of them. "Hmmm. These over here are way too skinny, but those are bigger. I don't know if they'd last long enough to do the job we need, though. We'll take them because they could replace arrows, if needed, with a little adaptation. We'll just see about a few arrowheads while we're here." Her ingenuity impressed the soldier.

They walked further down the aisles, and she continued. "Now, over here in the housewares section, most people left mop handles and toilet plungers behind. The handles are pretty thick for firing, though they could be jammed into a leg joint to totally disable those vehicles. The longer handles would need to be cut off to be easily used. The plunger handles are just right. All of them could certainly cripple a walker!"

Saul remembered reels of World War Two fighting, where people would run up to enemy tanks and lob grenades at them. That shredded the treads and stopped the tank or killed the people inside. It was a time-tested tactic. He delved into more of what he remembered from his high school history classes. "What if we made something bigger than a crossbow, like a ballista? Do you think that would work?"

Ariella gave him a big smile. "Somebody remembers his studies! Not a bad idea, though something that size couldn't be pulled through the snow easily. We'll have to think on it," she told him.

Saul gave her an equally large grin. "I'm so glad that a beautiful woman like you said 'we' and included me."

They couldn't get lost in each other for long because it could be dangerous to linger. The group headed out with their chosen weapons and a number of mop handles. Valerie wanted some of the handles, too. "They can be used as splints for broken bones, if necessary." They came upon some hard bars of soap, useful for laundry. "These are good for tanning hides, as well. They also come in handy to clean off after exposure to poison ivy," the EMT said, grabbing them.

Before they left, they also picked up a few remaining masks, originally intended for use when sanding. They'd do well to filter the particulates in the air. "Once the available manufactured masks are gone, we'll have to resort to sewing strips of fabric together as best we can," Valerie told them.

When they were outside the store, Valerie asked Saul. "How do the cooks heat their meals? If they just use wood fires, then maybe something like that old food truck over there might work, if it can be repaired. If the inside area still functions, it could wind up being time-saving and more fuel efficient. What do you think?" She pointed to a run-down and sad-looking food truck that had been abandoned near the parking lot of the building.

"It could still work, especially for those who don't have any means to cook. Undoubtedly it'll need some repairs, but if they aren't too extensive, our mechanics might be able to deal with it and get it working," Saul agreed. "We can't haul it today; we've got too many people and too much stuff as it is, but I'll make a note to have a mechanic and a couple people with some horses come out. If it's repairable, they can haul it to our encampment."

"By the way," the EMT said as another thought occurred to her, "do you think we could stop at the firehouse we passed? They might have an ambulance we could use. Even if it doesn't work, any medical equipment in the place would be useful in the triage area."

Saul liked the way these two women thought. "I can see the future holds a journey to plunder any hospitals we can reach, as well!"

The expedition was in luck. There was an ambulance with some equipment. Other medical gear they found in the building was placed inside it. The truck had enough gas left in the tank to make it back to the little settlement.

When Saul got back, he told Jason about what they'd found. The two made another report to their command. "The area is now more fortified. We've organized people with weapons experience for defense. We've got a kitchen area being built and we're working on cooking capability. Soon we'll begin to be able to more efficiently feed the hungry community. We've started to pick up whatever medical instruments and supplies we can find to heal our wounded. Our future is looking a little more secure now."

***

Summer ripened into fall, and the inhabitants of the makeshift little town harvested what they had grown. The food was stored to get them through the winter. By that time it was obvious that Saul and Ariella had become a couple. When the last of the fruits and vegetables had been brought into the communal kitchen, and whatever further edibles that could be foraged had been found, people gathered to observe the end of a successful harvest and celebrate together to honor the happy couple.

Saul laughed, "I don't know if this is an engagement celebration or a wedding ceremony. Maybe we should just call it a pairing party! By the way, when can we plan an event for you and Valerie?"

Jason laughed self-consciously. "Let's just deal with yours, for now!"

Jason noticed Valerie standing nearby. She had heard Saul's comment and had turned to leave the party. He gave a quick frown to Saul for making her uncomfortable and joined her.

"Don't let my buddy bother you," Jason said softly to her, attempting to make her feel better.

Valerie took his hand and led him into the cool night air. Turning to him, she opened her mouth. She tried to speak, but failed.

Jason kept her hand in his. With his free hand, he smoothed her hair back from her eyes. "Whatever you have to say, just take your time and tell me," he urged her.

"You know, Saul and Ariella clicked from the start. They had no hesitation, like there isn't anything bad that might happen." She blew out a breath and continued, "I've seen people die, and it kills me knowing that I might have saved them with the right equipment and medicine. I just don't know… Do we dare think of a future?" She looked at him, and he saw the turmoil in her face. "I have feelings for you, and we're good together. Does that make it right to bring children into this, knowing the dangers? There are so many things they won't have. What about all the diseases I won't be able to cure? I want to do what I can for the people who need me, but what happens when it's beyond my skill?"

"We'll work it out together," Jason said, and held her close. "I certainly don't have a crystal ball. We face an uncertain future, where all we can do is our best. All we've got is ourselves and our determination. I'll make you this promise; I'll try to make each day together a good one. All I know is, I need you there beside me."

He gently placed his hands around her face and said, "What do you say? Together we can do this." The kiss they shared was their answer to each other.

***

Winter came, and the ferocity of the lake effect weather became evident. The temperature plummeted. Riders on horseback occasionally had a hard time getting through the snow and wagons were often unusable. It became clear that walkers couldn't advance easily as the ice became more prevalent.

Jason decided, "We should create more ice by watering down areas on the outskirts of the town to thwart their attacks."

***

Many times through the winter, walkers fell on the ice and couldn't get back up. The operators had to abandon the machines and slog through the snow to get away. Intrepid hunters snowshoed over to the vacant vehicles and studied them.

Saul took their information to all the defenders of the village. "Try to target their optics, as well as joints. Those seem to be the most vulnerable areas."

Over the winter, the cooks were hard-pressed to make their provisions last and give people something warm to sustain them. The soups began to be more watery.

"People are beginning to get sick. Their caloric needs aren't being met, and I'm concerned about making what medicine I have last through the winter months." Valerie was caring for some older people who weren't doing too well in the cold, lean times. She was also caring for a pregnant woman. Ariella was pregnant, too, and Valerie wanted to make sure the two women delivered healthy babies. The scarcity of food was the problem, and there were no prenatal vitamins to be found.

Worried for Ariella, Saul had gone far afield, sometimes by himself, to try to find vitamins, medicine and food, with no luck.

Jason knew Valerie was concerned. "We're going to have to travel further to see if there might be any provisions that can still be found." Using a couple tracked vehicles, he and a few of the defenders traveled close to what had been Wright-Patterson Air Force Base.

Jason had done that deliberately. "I want to have what will hopefully be a safe stopping spot to rest before we head back." While there, he met up with a few soldiers who still had some communication equipment. "Let me see if I can contact command and make a report," he said. When handed the equipment, he tried contacting his superiors a few times, with no success. He was discouraged to think that they all might be dead.

Jason endeavored to carry on. "Well, at least let me pass on some intelligence to you so you can pass it on to your people. We've found the walkers don't do well in deep snow or on ice. Also, the hinges of their jointed legs and their optics are vulnerable to attack. All we can do so far is wedge hardwood stakes into the joints, but it seems effective enough."

The soldiers from the base agreed that the information was valuable. They were able to share a little ammunition, but not much. Jason and his crew were grateful for whatever could be contributed. Nothing was manufactured anymore.

Jason had a lot to think about on their way back to their little town. As they came upon the perimeter of their settlement, they heard the characteristic metallic whine of walkers. The repeating echo of gunfire followed the alien vehicles as they lumbered around and tried to break through the fortified outer barrier of useless vehicles.

Jason's adrenaline kicked in. "Here, take the ATV left and try to outmaneuver them." The hunter nodded his understanding and moved to get the vehicle going. Jason moved to talk to the hunters in the other ATV. "Go around to the right and keep them from surrounding the town."

"Where are you going?" one of the hunters asked.

"I've got to get close enough to them to do damage. Obviously the settlement's firepower isn't doing enough."

Running across the snow slowed Jason down, but he powered through the best he could. The ATVs were to the left and right of the Xanites. The aliens couldn't surround the settlement any further, so he went down the middle. Thinking quickly, he picked up some sturdy limbs and broke them into usable lengths. "I'll jam these into joints if I can. I'll use my ammunition to try to disable their optics if I get the chance at a clear shot," he thought as adrenaline and worry spurred him forward.

While one particularly bold walker was focused on an ATV, he ran up and jammed a branch into one of the legs. He ducked away before it could fire at him. Taking aim, he disabled the optics. "That one is slowed down," Jason said, exhaling heavily in the frosty air.

That first walker slowly moved away from the barrier and tried to make its way to the surrounding woods. Before it could get too far, the damaged leg gave out and the alien inside was forced to leave it.

The gangly being watched the hunters, who had moved to attack it.

"Shouldn't we go after this one?" the hunters asked Jason.

"Just leave it! Focus on the town!" Jason yelled at them.

Once the alien saw that it wasn't going to be pursued, it quickly left, looking back questioningly at the humans.

Before Jason could do anything else, the second walker continued its attack. It finally broke through the barrier protecting the town's inhabitants.

As people were busy trying to attack the walker, it careened through one of the rough buildings. Townspeople were too focused on finishing the rampaging alien vehicle to worry about anything else. They didn't realize, until too late, that the structure was beginning to fall. The walker was slowed when both hind legs were paralyzed, but it kept crawling with the front legs in a desperate bid to get through to the other side of the building.

The collapse of the walls and roof caused the wood-burning stove inside to crack. The scattered embers set fire to the wooden frame. The walker was trapped inside the blazing building. People tried unsuccessfully to douse the flames. Nobody wanted to think of the fate of the alien trapped inside.

The fire began to spread to the nearby medical building where Valerie worked. Jason knew that there was nothing he could do for the other structure. His mind was on trying to rescue Valerie and anyone else still in the medical building. He ran in and assessed the situation. Internally, he wasn't as cool as he seemed outwardly.

Ariella was already trying to help someone out of the building. She was having problems with the bigger person. Saul ran over to assist her. He was worried for her and their unborn child. They didn't want the smoke harming their baby. Together, they got the patient out quickly. "Stay here – try to help others who get out!" he instructed her when he knew she'd be safe.

Coughing, Jason sped through the flames, looking around for anyone else unable to get out. He noticed a couple older people on cots. He helped one patient up while still searching for Valerie. Fortunately, just then Saul ran back in. Jason handed the frail patient over to him.

"Have you seen Valerie? Take that person out of here. There is still one more patient to move."

Frantically, Jason searched through the smoke and found Valerie slumped on the ground. He ran over to her and picked her up.

Saul assisted the last victim, but he noted the anxiety on Jason's face.

By the time the two men got Valerie and the last patient out, the guys had gotten pretty singed. The medical center would need repairs and the other structure was totally gone.

"At least we stopped the attack," Jason said, once he was outside for the last time. His lips were dry and his clothes were charred, but he had only a few minor burns and a sore throat.

Valerie had been on the ground, so she hadn't been scorched. Once she regained consciousness, she insisted on taking over medical duties. "I'm relieved that none of the injuries are worse," she reported. "Besides smoke inhalation, most wounds are from battling the walkers, not the flames."

Going into full EMT mode, she fussed over her guy. "Almost losing you makes me think that you might be worth keeping around," she teased, smiling. At his look she insisted, "Get used to it, because I'm going to take care of you from now on. Someone has to look out for you, you crazy, heroic guy!"

Saul and Ariella noticed the newly confirmed couple's quiet comments to each other. "So, it looks like another pairing party will need to be planned!" Saul didn't mind making his good friend squirm a little, now that they all were safe.

"It took you two long enough," Ariella chimed in with happiness for her two friends.

At first, Jason seemed a bit taken aback at the thought of a public sharing of his feelings.

"I know you're very private, but you'll get used to it," Valerie told him. Then the congratulatory grins on Saul's and Ariella's faces mirrored the loving smiles on Jason's and Valerie's.

***

"This winter has certainly been long and hard. The community has had to come together to do some quick repairs to the triage building so it could continue to be used." Saul talked about the obvious things to keep Jason's mind from the upcoming midwinter celebration. This year, they would combine the winter festivities with Jason and Valerie's pairing party.

Due to the destruction of the other building, there wasn't space to comfortably house as many people. Overcrowding caused flared tempers at times. Being so close together also caused outbreaks of flu to increase. Everyone was kept busy filling in and keeping the community functioning.

Ariella was due to deliver her baby in the spring. Valerie had a hard time keeping her stubborn friend away from people as much as possible to keep her from getting sick. Ariella was intent on helping as much as possible. Unfortunately, the other mother-to-be had recently died during birth. The inhabitants were saddened by the loss of both the mother and child. So far, there had not been many pregnancies and all the townsfolk insisted on celebrating any births as a renewal of hope for the future.

***

Spring's new growth eased the people's memories of the previous harsh winter. The walker attacks continued to taper off. No one knew why that was.

Saul and Ariella's child was born healthy and strong. Everyone was heartened by the addition of the new baby and happily planned a welcome party.

Valerie wasn't sure if she should make it known that she was pregnant now, as well. She and Jason discussed the pros and cons through many evenings together.

Jason, of course, wasn't so eager to share their news with absolutely everyone. "Why does everybody else have to know our business?"

"To me, it boils down to a choice between telling them now and giving people something to look forward to, or waiting and seeing how things go. After all, in a few months' time, it'll be obvious anyway," Valerie said, taking a logical approach.

Jason thought about it and proposed, "How about we compromise and wait for a while? Then, sometime before it becomes obvious anyway, certain others can be told." He was reluctant to share the dark realization that, in these conditions, it wasn't as sure a thing as it had been in the days of hospitals and medicine.

Valerie saw the reason in waiting and agreed. "That could work. After all, that way people won't have to wait as long for the delivery. However, I'm going to need Ariella's help with a few things, so she'll need to know."

"Help with what?" Jason wasn't sure what that might entail.

"Well, I'm going to need maternity clothes, first. Then I'll need baby clothes. Just little things like that. We'll have to think of baby names, too. After all, we can't call the child 'hey, you'!"

The two knew that, once Ariella was told, Saul would also find out. The two longtime buddies were sharing a local attempt at a barley beer when Jason revealed to Saul some misgivings he had.

"Look at how bad last winter was. True, the attacks seem to have lessened for some reason, but I have to admit that the thought of putting Valerie through this scares me. What if something bad happens during the birth? If she needs surgery, she can't do it for herself. We've got very little medicine or medical expertise available."

Saul started making a response when Jason continued, pacing in his agitation. "The lack of medicine is scary enough, but Valerie and I hesitated to bring a child into this situation because we know that, for the next couple generations or so, things are going to be extremely rough. Do we dare inflict this on them?"

Saul waited for his friend to take a breath. "We're here to help each other, buddy. Together we'll teach them to be tough. We'll show them how to survive. Yes, we may think things are backward right now, yet this is really no different than the settlers in the movement west. We are the repositories of a lot of knowledge, and we need to pass that information on. Who else are we going to pass that on to, if not our kids? You and I, together with the other Green Berets, will share our training and provide the next generation with the tools and instruction that they will need to make a better life for themselves."

The two shared a few moments of silence where much went unsaid. Saul continued his response. "This is our mission – to help rebuild society. You wonder if the hardship is worth it. If we can accomplish this goal, we help our children and grandchildren for generations into the future. With my child just born and you with one on the way, of course it's worth it! Together, we're going to make damn sure things get better for them. This is not going to be the end. Not of society and certainly not of the knowledge we can give them! This is what we've been trained to do, and this is what we're going to do!"

With renewed resolution, they raised their glasses of beer at that promise and toasted the unknown future.

The Food Truck with Teeth

The early morning sunlight emphasized the demolished and ragged skyline of the nearby abandoned city. Ash billowing from the many burned-out buildings was visible for miles. In the settlement built outside the decayed ruins, Bethany hurried along. The dust and exertion made it hard for her to breathe. So many unwashed bodies didn't make it any more pleasant, either.

She puffed as she rushed through the crowds milling around the tents and makeshift shacks that formed the main market. Some people were desperately trying to sell or barter whatever they had gotten their hands on for another day's food or shelter. Others were urgently trying to find the medicine that would let them survive a little longer.

"Today's haul has been really good, compared to some days." It was a satisfactory accomplishment. She knew she had to return quickly to her food truck. "My very full backpack could invite getting robbed." She'd spent her barter goods and scrip, so she couldn't afford to replace her hard-gained purchases if they were stolen.

Her gaunt frame was swallowed up in the clothing that used to fit closer to her body. The various rips and stains were testaments to the scrapes she had gotten herself out of successfully.

"With my backpack and shaggy hair, people won't look at me as being any different than any other displaced refugee," she reasoned.

She quickly moved out of the way as one unhappy customer started yelling and waving his arms. The buyer hadn't expected costs to increase so dramatically.

"As demand goes up, prices rise to match. We're all trying to survive the upheaval caused by the Xanite invasion," she realized.

She still kept looking over her shoulder. She knew she had to take a winding route back to her truck. To stay safe, she had to throw off anyone who might try to hurt her. Worse, she didn't dare lead any "acquirers" back to the food truck. People like that were known to kidnap victims to be put to work in some hard labor camp. She shuddered at the thoughts of what else they were known to do. Some of them would find young, healthy people for wealthy clients' depraved desires.

"I just hope Tai and the truck will be at the right spot to meet me," she worried. Her assistant was young and less knowledgeable about the evil some people could inflict. He could also get caught up in some piece of new tech and easily lose track of time.

Bethany noticed she was getting a lot of unwanted attention from a couple guys who were loitering nearby. She sped up her pace as she ducked down yet another busy lane in the bazaar.

She hurried, hoping to elude the two predators. The two overly interested thugs casually loped through the throngs to follow her, but she knew her way through this maze of shops. She slipped around the corner of a nearby vendor just as the two men started down the alleyway.

She sprinted to the food truck, which she saw just ahead. "It's about time you showed up," she said with a relieved sigh.

Tai shook his close-cropped head and turned his gaze from what he was doing to peer at her questioningly. "We're right on time. What's the prob–"

"Just get us out of here. I was followed," she said urgently, cutting him off.

The young guy moved his short, skinny frame to get into the van. She lithely followed him. The truck sped away, controlled by the artificial intelligence. The two human passengers trusted the computer to get them far away from the two hoodlums, and they knew the AI could do it more safely than most humans could manage.

Bethany and Tai did their best to hang on while they made their way to the back. The computer increased the speed of the vehicle. The young woman hauled the backpack with her treasures onto a counter to show Tai what she'd purchased.

The truck lurched unexpectedly. "What's going on?" Bethany called to the computer.

"Just a bit of a roadblock, but we're past it now." The AI sounded pleased with itself.

"I think this should be enough to keep this food truck venture going for a while. So, what shall we call ourselves? By the way, has the AI decided on a name?"

"Yeah, it's a toss-up at this point between two automotive-related terms. He mentioned a name like Fender or something, if I recall."

"I don't know what to say to that," she said, bewildered.

Tai's focus flitted to the next item he found. "Mushrooms," he said, looking at them appreciatively. "Where did you get these? Are you sure they're safe?"

Bethany answered him briskly, "I am sure of the source, so they're safe. And, no, I won't tell you who my supplier is, but he's reliable. He doesn't want to lose clients by accidentally poisoning them. However, if you're not convinced, we could let you try one to find out."

She gave him a little nudge to show it was a joke. Before her partner could rattle off more questions, Bethany brought out the other things she had purchased. "Take a look at these," she said proudly. "Onions and peppers! I even found some cheese! We can make tacos!"

"Yeah, if only we had tortillas," Tai said wistfully.

"We do," Bethany said proudly and pulled out a stack of already made tortillas from another portion of the backpack.

"Now we just need some hamburger," Tai said longingly.

"Too hard to get, but I did get some chicken. Will that do?" Bethany looked pleased with herself. Her young assistant nodded as they returned to the cab of the truck to sit down.

"So, do I understand you've chosen Fender as your name?" she asked the AI.

"No. I told Tai at least ten times, it's Axle, not Fender. Fender sounds like a bumper car and I am not some amusement park ride for children!" The masculine-sounding synthetic voice spoke in displeased tones at the perceived slight. "Really, you must need a memory module upgrade. My service as an armed forces supply truck may be over, but I still consider myself military grade. I didn't mind when you modified the back portion for cooking, or when you painted me. At least you didn't reconfigure my weaponry. While I am forever grateful for being rescued from the junkyard, I deserve a serious name that fits."

"So, you don't want to be called Grill or Lug Nut or something?" Tai joked. He could really step in it at times.

"Functioning as a food truck is well within my capabilities. I deserve to be taken seriously. In fact, I'll have you know that I…"

Bethany prepared herself for the usual litany of stories she'd heard before. When the dash radio interrupted the AI's latest rendition, she was glad for the reprieve.

An unfamiliar voice came through the receiver. "Hello. I'm looking for anyone who might have some culinary experience. If you have any background at all, I would like to have a word with you."

She looked at Tai, but he seemed as apprehensive as she was. This wasn't directed specifically at them, but it was still worrying. "And just who are you? Why are you sending out an unsolicited broadcast that all can hear?" she knew the voice activated system would convey her words.

"I'm Bobby Slay. I'm a chef, in case you haven't heard of me," the man said, as if he expected his name to mean something to her.

"Should the name be familiar?" She didn't want to give this guy any advantage. "You should know this is a dangerous way to do recruiting." She was unconcerned that she was being unfriendly. If it turned out he really was who he claimed to be, she could always apologize later.

"I'm in desperate need of an experienced sous-chef, and they're in short supply. This is my last-ditch effort to find one." He jumped right into the attributes that he was trying to find. "I need someone who is a really good problem solver and acquirer. If you're proficient at procuring things that are hard to find, I could use that," Slay said pleasantly.

"I'm not an 'acquirer.'" She was offended at that term. "I don't rob. I trade. I won't do illegal stuff like kidnapping, or murder anybody, no matter how much they may deserve it," she said, still trying to figure out this guy's angle.

The laugh on the other end of the transmission was genuine. "No, I'm not asking you to do anything like stealing or killing. But if you're good at getting things, I could use your skills in finding some ingredients for me. And if you've got skills in the kitchen, that's even better!"

She scoffed. "If it's exotic spices or something, you're just totally out of luck. Most fancy stuff isn't grown anymore. You're really out of touch if you don't know that supply lines aren't long enough anymore for imports. If it isn't available locally, I can't get it."

"Do you think you might…" the man continued.

"Hold it. These frequencies aren't exactly very secure. We shouldn't even be discussing this kind of activity over the radio if we want to keep out of trouble and stay alive. And trust me, my team and I do want to continue living," she said emphatically, "so this conversation has to end now."

"All right, I can understand that. Can I just ask quickly if we could meet somewhere and discuss this further?" Slay hoped his persuasion would work.

"I don't know." She looked at Tai for his input. When he just shrugged his shoulders, she continued, "It seems too much like a trap."

"So far, you're the only one who has responded. We could meet somewhere of your choosing, if that makes you feel better," Slay cajoled.

"What will make it worth my while?" Bethany boldly questioned him.

"What would a tank of propane get me?"

"Make it two, and we can talk," Bethany countered.

"Are you sure about this?" Tai looked at her with worry.

It was Bethany's turn to shrug. "Well, we'll need more propane, and it'll save me some time trying to find it somewhere else, so it'll work out to our favor either way."

"So you'll do it?" Slay, who had heard her response to Tai, asked hopefully.

"Sure, why not," Bethany acquiesced. "I used to know this pizza place on the Northside, where they made those deep dish pies. Do you know it?" She hoped anyone else who might be listening wouldn't understand the reference.

"I remember that place. It was one of my favorites before the Xanites happened." Slay confirmed.

"Good. Then meet me there at dusk. Come alone and bring the two tanks of propane. If you don't have them, don't bother coming. If you're late, or you have people with you, we're out of there," she warned him.

"How about I bring just one person – a driver?" Slay asked.

"All right, but only one, and I'll be checking your vehicle," she said. Bethany made a slicing move at her throat which told Axle to end the transmission.

"Now what?" Axle asked.

"Well, now we wait, and meet with this Slay person at sundown." Bethany sincerely hoped her instincts were right about this guy.

***

Tai, Bethany and Axle pulled into the barren parking area of the run-down pizza place. It always hurt her to see these familiar places as they had become, then stop and picture them as they had once been. The parking lot had been well-tended and full, not weedy, cracked and deserted. The building, in her memories, had been in functioning shape and exuding wonderful, spicy smells. Now, there was only the smell of rot and ambient smoke blown in from the nearby city ruins.

Axle slowed down, but didn't stop. "Surely you don't want me to park in the middle of this area. That just screams 'target!' How about I park in the shadows and we wait for this guy to show up?"

"Good idea," Bethany agreed.

Soon, a luxurious electric sedan pulled into the parking lot and whirred to a stop. Despite herself, Bethany was impressed at the well-maintained vehicle. "Somebody must have money," she said. Axle and Tai stayed quiet and watched.

A middle-aged man got out of the passenger door. The driver stood up from behind the wheel and opened the trunk. Producing two propane tanks as promised, he placed them on the ground.

She actually sucked in a breath for a moment. "I recognize him!"

"Who is he?" Tai asked, indifferent to the obvious signs of status.

"I'm sure that's the guy I saw on TV a long time ago. A little older and a touch of gray, but it's definitely him. Just don't act like you're too impressed with him."

"Oh. OK. Shall we go?" Tai fingered a weapon that he rarely carried.

"I'll be ready, just in case," Axle assured them.

The two walked over to the sedan, keeping their hands in sight, but close to their guns.

"There you are," Bobby said jovially. "In the dark, I hadn't seen you."

Bethany let his remark remain unanswered, since not being seen was the idea. "Mind if I have a look at your car? I've never seen one in such good condition."

"Please do," Bobby said agreeably.

Once they were satisfied, Slay asked, "Would you give me a tour of your vehicle? I'd like to see it!"

"Go ahead," Tai said without thinking, then looked at Bethany. She just shrugged. Axle would keep an eye on this stranger.

"Tai and I will take the tanks over to the truck while you look. Then my assistant here can give you a tour."

Slay walked around the truck and whistled. "Gun turret on top. I can't wait to see inside."

"Nice!" Slay exclaimed as he and Tai came back down the steps after the tour. As the two walked around the front of the truck, the celebrity chef stopped and said, "What is this that I see here?"

He had directed the question to Bethany, as the one who seemed to be the leader, but she just looked at Tai and said, "Go ahead. You know you want to!"

Tai enthusiastically proclaimed, "I painted shark's teeth on the front because we can not only cook, we're tough enough to deal with whatever comes our way!"

"So what do you call yourselves?" Slay wanted to know.

Again, Tai spoke first. "We haven't quite decided yet. It might be something like 'Tactical Taco,' or something."

Slay laughed appreciatively. "That's good. How about just 'The Food Truck with Teeth'?"

Tai loved the name and was thrilled to be the center of the important stranger's attention. Bethany, however, wanted to get down to business. She felt vulnerable being in one place too long.

"Why don't you get the tanks stowed while he and I talk?" she suggested to Tai. He agreed to her request and got busy putting the propane cylinders away.

"So, it looks like you two can do pretty well for yourselves when it comes to getting provisions," Slay started. "Can you fill me in on your culinary background?"

"Well, I started out doing prep work. I had some culinary school training before the invasion, so at least I had some skills to draw on. Unfortunately, I hadn't been there long enough to learn much beyond the basics. When the Xanites arrived, people had to try to do what they could for themselves. I've always been a quick learner. At the restaurant where I started, they began to teach me what they could. After a while, positions needed to be filled. I picked up skills easily and moved up in the kitchen."

"Tell me about this advancement." Slay was curious to hear about it.

"People died or got kidnapped and had to be replaced. Others moved up and their previous job had to be filled. Newer people would start off doing the basic work and progress to the more complicated positions as they learned more skills. I eventually advanced to the spot that directly helped the chef."

"That's impressive," Slay said sincerely. "That would be called the sous-chef position in a traditional, high-end kitchen."

Bethany scoffed. "Maybe once upon a time there were what you call high-end kitchens, but now this is as high-end as most people are going to see. Why, I've even heard of people verifying that a food truck is going to be in a certain place at a specific time so they can plan a date. Pairing proposals have also taken place at these trucks because they're about the fanciest dining some local areas could provide in these circumstances!"

Slay thought for a brief moment. "You know, your abilities in the kitchen, and in getting the ingredients I'll need, would be valuable to me. Skills like that are hard to come by these days. I could use someone with your experience to assist me with an important function coming up. Do you think you could leave your food truck in your partner's hands and come to work for me for a while?"

Bethany needed a minute to think things over. "I suppose it's a possibility, if you really think you need my skills for this job. Just how important is this thing coming up? After all, Tai is good at the grill, but he isn't as adept at finding the ingredients. I'm the one with the contacts. Even so, it's getting harder and harder to find anything remotely edible."

She eyed him closely. "On the other hand, I'm sure someone with your standing has first choice of whatever is available. I'll bet you could probably keep him supplied with enough ingredients to last him till I return," Bethany wheedled.

Bobby nodded his head in understanding and laughed. "I like your style. I'll see what I can do to help your friend. I promise I'll get him something. Times are tough, but you have my word."

They shook hands. "For your first venture," Bobby said, "how about you see what you can do to get some cognac and some burgundy?"

"How much?" Bethany immediately asked.

The chef was impressed with her bravado. "I'll need one bottle of each. Full bottles, please, if you can. Unopened would be even better, so I'm assured they haven't been watered down."

Bethany nodded and queried, "Where do you want them delivered?"

"Just give me a call on the same frequency we spoke on before and I'll have somebody pick it up." He walked back to his sedan. The waiting driver briskly opened the door for the celebrity chef, and walked around to get behind the wheel again. In a whir, the car and the two people were gone.

Tai walked up to her and said, "Booze. Where are you going to find that?"

"I have my sources," she smiled confidently. She turned to the van to address the AI. "Axle, how are we doing for power and ammo?"

"I'm fully charged. I can go a couple hundred more miles before needing to recharge. I'm fully stocked with six thousand rounds of ammo. With those two propane tanks, we're good for a lot of cooking. Should that do for your purposes?"

She laughed in anticipation. "Let's go score the man some booze!"

They peeled out of the deserted parking lot and headed toward the seedier part of the ramshackle camp.

"Are you sure about this?" Tai was twitchy as he watched the bad part of the refugee area that was speeding past his window. The shadows increased. He was getting more nervous the darker the streets got.

"If the coordinates you gave me are correct, we're almost there," Axle said.

Bethany shook her head and muttered, "Why do you always figure I've made a mistake?"

"Well, that *is* why it's called *human* error, isn't it?" Axle sounded so sanctimonious that Tai laughed.

Before anything else could be said, Axle guided the vehicle to a stop in front of a very dark and foreboding building.

"Wait close by in the shadows," Bethany told her partner and the AI. She quietly got out of the truck and walked quickly down the side of the building into the gloom. Her two friends watched with apprehension as she disappeared into the darkness.

***

Bethany slipped around the building to the back, where there was an entrance hidden behind some old wood and bricks. Hidden to all, that is, but those who knew where it was located. She gave a special set of raps and waited for someone to open the door.

"What do you want?" someone she'd never seen before challenged her.

"I'm here to sell cookies," she replied, using the preset phrase.

"Really? What kind?" was the response.

"Just get your boss," she said, growing annoyed that this guy wasn't following the coded protocols.

Before the man could even turn around, the underling's employer appeared in the inner doorway. "I'll take care of this," the formidable woman said. Just a look shooed the subordinate away. Giving a slight smile to Bethany, the serious and graying woman said, "Hard to find good help these days." She then asked, "And to what do I owe this infrequent visit?"

Bethany took that as an invitation to enter.

Once they were inside, the matriarch motioned for Bethany to sit down and talk. When they both were comfortable, she opened up to the powerful woman. "You know how difficult things are. After all, you hear every bit of gossip in the community. Even if you aren't directly involved, you know what goes on almost before it happens."

"Yes, that is true. Just as I know you've been skirting some of the local acquirers. You do need to be more careful, you know. And tell me, just who was it you met with tonight?"

Bethany stiffened slightly, being careful to hide it because she didn't want to give away too much. Instead, she decided to dissemble a little to find out what the older woman knew.

"Well, I've been with Axle and Tai, but then, you know that."

The matriarch asked, "I know about Tai. Who is this Axle, though?"

Bethany relaxed a little bit because this was information she could share.

"Axle is the name the truck's AI has chosen to be called."

"I see. Axle is an unusual name. But you haven't answered my question. Who is the person you and Tai and Axle met with earlier?" the matriarch asked again, showing some displeasure with Bethany's evasions.

The younger woman hesitated for a minute, trying to decide how much she could divulge.

The commanding woman then asked Bethany, "While you think of an answer, do you want something to drink?"

It suddenly popped into Bethany's head that this was her opening.

"Do you have any cognac or burgundy? I could use some of either of those. Actually, both, if you can spare them."

"You never were much of a drinker. Why do you want alcohol now?" the powerful matron began to ask, but before any answer could be given, a huge crash was heard in the front part of the building.

"Go! Now!" the matriarch ordered, and the younger woman sped out the back door just as a Xanite mechanized vehicle crashed through the front wall. Its four articulated legs weren't stopped long by the wreckage of the old building.

Bethany could hear the bursts of a machine gun and hoped it was Tai up on top of the truck.

"If you've come out of the shadows, things are bad. Try to distract the aliens just long enough, because I need to get back inside to help." Bethany formulated a plan as quickly as she could. She pulled out her gun and ran back into the room she had just left. Mesmerized, she watched the vehicle bend its weirdly shaped legs lower to allow a couple aliens to step out. She was only able to get a clear shot at one. It took just one shot and it was dead. The other was under attack by the matriarch's men and that intruder was soon killed, as well. She didn't take the time to stop and notice what the aliens' blood looked like.

The fighting was quickly over. The matron approached Bethany. Surrounded by her guards, the matriarch looked formidable. "Surely you didn't lead these creatures here," she said in a stern and ominous tone.

Bethany paused to recall their trip to this building. If she had been talking to anyone else, Bethany's first response would have been to mouth off. However, in deference to the matriarch's clout and to lessen the older woman's unhappy mood, she toned her attitude down.

"Axle certainly would have pointed out if we were followed. He would also know if any drones were nosing around because of their transmissions. Please allow me to ask him," she politely requested. When the matriarch nodded, she got out her radio.

"Axle, did you notice anyone following us here? Were there any communications to indicate we were being monitored?" Bethany began. When Axle replied in the negative, she turned to the matriarch again.

The influential matron seemed more placated. “Very well, since it doesn’t seem that you led them here, then there is the deeper question of how they found the hideout.”

Axle urgently broke in over the radio, “It looks like whatever business you’re conducting needs to be finished soon. We have some street-to-street activity.”

The matriarch gathered herself and continued, “With that question answered, what was it you came to ask me? Ah, yes. You asked for cognac and burgundy.”

Bethany knew it was now or never. “It would be appreciated. Alcohol is impossible to find. That was why the person came to see me. He wanted it for some important function.”

The matriarch thought for a moment, then came to a decision. “You may have it. As a matter of fact, I will give you a bottle of each, since it seems to be so essential.”

The powerful woman made a motion for an underling to retrieve the bottles.

With her audience coming to an end, Bethany had one last request of the influential matron. “You’ve helped me so much already, but may I request that you keep an eye on Axle and Tai? You know that I’m better at getting out of trouble than they are!”

The powerful woman looked at Bethany and smiled. “What makes you think I haven’t been looking out for you three?”

The underling returned with the bottles. The matriarch passed them to Bethany, speaking the traditional words. “Remember, someday I will be owed something from you.”

Bethany stood there and received the heavy containers, which had survived the attack. “I will not forget,” she said, using the formal reply. “For loyalty and tradition, I owe you and will repay.” Just before Bethany turned to go, she said, “Thank you, Great-Aunt.”

***

Back in the truck, the three were silent for quite a while. The precious bottles had been carefully stowed, and Axle was driving speedily away from the scene of the fighting.

The AI broke into their musings. "Just to keep you notified, it seems that the aliens aren't advancing very fast. Armed neighborhood groups are resisting and aren't allowing the intruders to get a permanent foothold in the area."

Tai was unusually quiet, but he kept casting side glances that began to vex the young woman.

"What's your problem?" Bethany couldn't take any more of his curious looks.

"Was that lady really your great-aunt?" Tai blurted out.

"How do you know about that?" she demanded.

"We both heard you over the radio. You didn't hit the mute button," Axle reminded her.

"Well, yes and no. It's complicated. She has power and authority, and it's a title that shows respect. It doesn't necessarily denote any genetic relationship."

"You said you were going to owe her. What is that debt going to be?" Tai persisted.

"That is yet to be determined."

"It sounds almost like 'The Godfather.' I've found references to that societal hierarchy online." Axle was proud of his knowledge.

"Have you been doing more internet searches? I've told you about plugging yourself into some unknown and possibly infected site where you don't belong. I worry about your health and well-being, you know!" Bethany knew how important Axle was to their team.

"You do realize that my defense-ware is military grade, and it's as up to date as I can keep it. Besides, you don't need to be telling *me* about protection. You both seem to get infected with colds and flu all the time. You rarely wear masks, and you frequently wear them wrong," Axle quipped.

"Yeah, well, do you remember when somebody tried to hack into your system and your voice began to sound feminine?" Bethany was glad to joke a little and lighten the mood.

When Axle sputtered to find a response, the young woman said, "Maybe it's about time to send a message to that guy that we have the goods." She wanted to get the group back to the business at hand.

"Uh, I'd hold off on that, if I were you," Axle told her. "We've got radio traffic about something going on ahead. It sounds serious." He paused then said, "Get everything stowed as fast as possible. NOW! We're about to have company."

Just before Tai could order the computer to play the transmissions, Axle yelled, "Incoming!" The AI swerved wildly to the other side of the road and sped up dramatically. A laser blast exploded not far from where they had been. The concussion and debris caused the truck to fishtail, but the computer kept it steady.

"What's going on?" Bethany asked her two companions, but neither had answers. Just ahead they all could see a mixture of Canadian and American trucks and troops fighting alongside some lesser-equipped volunteers. The humans were arrayed against some walking vehicles like the one that had destroyed the old building where Bethany met the matriarch.

"The bad guys have armored multi-environment vehicles with mounted guns. Some of their soldiers have airborne capability. I don't know about you, but I think that puts our guys at a bit of a disadvantage, and I don't like that," Axle said. "How about I pull onto that trail over there and flank them?"

"Can you get through there?" Tai asked doubtfully.

"I keep telling you, I *am* military grade. Even a transport truck has to be able to get where it needs to go. Just watch me." With that, Axle veered over and onto the dirt track leading behind the enemy.

The two cooks had been through this routine before. They quickly got everything put away and hurried to the cab to strap in before Axle did any extreme maneuvers.

"Can you get up top to the machine gun?" Bethany asked Tai.

"I wouldn't recommend it. Things are going to get rough," Axle warned as they bounced around.

"I know, but I'll try to be quick," Tai said with determination. He put on a headset and crawled out the door. After a try or two, he grabbed the ladder to get to the top of the vehicle.

"I'm tying myself in so you can maneuver, Axle. The ammunition is being loaded now, so give me a minute and I'll see what I can do about these guys."

"I'm positioning us to put the invaders in between us and the defenders," Axle informed them. The beings in the walking units hadn't paid much attention to the newcomer. They didn't think a food truck was dangerous and they continued to engage the defenders.

Once the truck was stopped, Tai was able to finish loading the gun. He began to shoot at the aliens. That made the enemy turn to face the new threat. Tai kept his bursts down to a few well-placed rounds at a time. "Take that!" he could be heard yelling in between shots. "Be careful," he warned his friends. "There are some aliens trying to sneak closer."

Bethany moved to the back of the vehicle and stood to one side of an open window. From that protected position, she could aim her shotgun at any attackers hiding from Tai. She looked out the window to assess the situation. "They're trying to surround us, but I've got this side," she spoke into her own mic.

"I'll take care of that," Axle said, and revved his motor. The truck swerved into a bunch of the bad guys who were trying to jump onto the vehicle on the opposite side of Bethany's position. "Let me introduce myself," Axle said sarcastically to them.

Soon more aliens, flying some strange one-being platforms, began attacking. "They're going to try boarding us," Axle called.

"I see them," Tai said quickly. "They're attempting to land on the roof." He pulled out his pistol to deal with the short-range targets and save the machine gun ammunition. Once he initialized the computer-guided mechanism for the turret, he could come back inside to relative safety while Axle took over. The young man moved to the back to cover the other side of the truck and help Bethany.

After a while, helicopters arrived and started chasing the aerial threat. The aliens' flying mechanisms gave them more maneuverability. The Xanites too often evaded the defenders' missiles. The humans couldn't afford to waste precious resources. However, the helicopters' machine guns were ideally suited to fighting the flying menace. When the aliens' airborne maneuvers were curtailed, they begin to disperse.

"They're an opportunistic bunch of hyena droppings, just attacking when and where they think we're weak." Tai was riding high on the adrenaline rush.

"We probably shouldn't stay long. They may come back." Bethany said, drained from the night's activities.

"We have company," Axle told them. "Night vision cameras show that they're approaching with their weapons at their sides and arms out. They are stopping a few yards away, so I don't think they're going to attack."

These were the defenders, who had come to look at the food truck that had helped them. They expressed their gratitude at the timely assistance.

Still riding an emotional wave, Tai said enthusiastically, "We're where we belong – helping to defeat the aggressors!"

Bethany smiled back at his enthusiasm.

***

The thanks from the human defenders meant a lot to Bethany and Tai. Axle took it all in stride. The two human companions were exhausted. "We still have to deliver these bottles of liquor, though," Bethany yawned.

"Can't we do that tomorrow?" Tai was willing to put anything off, if he could.

"No. We need to deliver the goods and get paid. Pay today means more shopping can be done tomorrow," Bethany answered.

They used the same radio frequency to contact Slay. On the other end someone responded, "Be at the same rendezvous place where you met before. Someone will meet you within about an hour. Will that be all right?"

Bethany replied that it would, since they were almost there. The two tired humans were dozing when the whir of a car made them stir. The two friends cautiously looked out the window to see Slay himself get out and walk over to them.

Bethany grabbed one bottle and gave the other to Tai to carry over to the celebrity. She wanted the kid to share in the good feelings of accomplishment, since it had been a shared venture to pick up the booze.

"You actually got some? And so soon? I'm amazed. I can't imagine where you found it!" Slay was impressed with their achievement in this time when most things were hard to find.

Before Tai could give away any information, Bethany got his attention and spoke up quickly. "For security's sake, I don't give away my sources."

"Security?" Tai asked. She gave a meaningful glare to him to indicate he shouldn't give away anything. Fortunately, the youngster caught on to her signal.

"Yes, for you, me and them. It's better this way." Bethany hoped there wouldn't be any further prying.

"I see," the important man said. "I have my own sources, and I can understand the situation. For similar reasons, I can't go into detail, but I want to convey my deepest thanks to the both of you. This is going to be very helpful."

The famous chef thought for a moment. "Are you two sure you wouldn't want to assist me in my kitchen? I could use the help with an important dinner. It's for a really good cause that could wind up helping a lot of people."

Tai backed toward the safety of the interior of the truck. Looking at Bethany he said, "Fancy gigs aren't for me. Go if you want to, but I feel more comfortable staying here."

"For a good cause, you say?" Bethany couldn't help her curiosity. She also couldn't resist the urge to help if she could.

Slay jumped on the question. "Yes, you would be helping me and the team I'm assembling. This has the potential to help ease a lot of humanity's suffering. Wouldn't that be a good thing?"

"How long would I have to be away? And who would take care of Axle and Tai?" she asked.

"I really don't need anyone to take care of me," Axle interjected, offended at the idea.

"Of course not, but I want to know you both will be safe and will have supplies," Bethany said to placate the touchy AI.

"I might be able to assist them with that," Slay conceded.

Bethany agreed. "I'll do it, but only if it isn't going to be for too long," she said.

"This cooking job would be a matter of two or three weeks. Certainly no more than a month. Your help would be valuable to a successful outcome." Slay turned to go back to the car, where the driver was waiting for him. "Now, if only I could source some decent vegetables. They might prove useful."

"I've got those," Bethany said proudly. She motioned for Tai to go get them.

"You're going to do great! This is going to open up a whole new way of life for you. Hopefully, for all of us," the famous chef said enigmatically, and the two got in the car.

Bethany waved at Tai and Axle, knowing they would be safe and she'd be back soon with more experiences to use in their cooking adventures.

Molybdenum Chef

An angry red sun set over the desolate landscape of the American southwest. Years of war with an invading alien horde, known as the Xanites, had left particulates in the atmosphere which added to the temperature extremes and the baleful color of the skies. Camouflaged in an undisclosed location of the inhospitable desert, a covert military complex remained hidden.

"Ladies and gentlemen, your attention, please!" The harried government official stood at the front of the group assembled at the hidden base. His off-the-rack suit had seen better days. That was the norm, since most manufacturing capability had been destroyed by the aliens.

Once the assembled culinary people settled down, the speaker continued. "I ask for your understanding in the convoluted and secretive way you were brought here. We couldn't risk having you injured or killed in a Xanite attack or targeted by human protesters in an attempt to thwart these proceedings."

The audience voiced concern, but the experienced speaker got their attention again. "As you all are aware, our war with the alien invaders has seen half the Earth's population killed and wreaked havoc on most countries' infrastructure. The combined Earth military has, at least, brought the advancement of their forces to a standstill. If this war continues, that won't last long, though. Time is of the essence."

Through the murmur of the assembled kitchen crews, one voice rose above the others. "Everything was so guarded that we weren't allowed to talk to others or see where we were going. Where are we? I'm sure we'd all like to know the answer to that," she said, looking around at the others seated in the auditorium. Like her, everyone was dressed in clean food service whites.

"Yes, Chef Marta Steward, I'm sure you all have questions. I'll get to them, if you'll let me," the aggravated civil servant stated firmly. "There have been some high-level meetings between the Xanites and the United Nations. They have finally agreed to sit down to talks with the human delegation. Maybe they just want time for reinforcements, or it could mean they don't want to commit more resources to this war."

At the agitation of the crowd, the speaker continued. "Most countries don't have the facilities or remaining organization to deal with the proposed talks with the aliens. It was a toss-up between a secret Russian facility and this complex. That site wound up being almost completely destroyed in a recent attack. It's unclear at this point if it was the Xanites or a human raid. That means it's up to us. We will host the aliens here because this base is one of the few remaining that can provide the necessary security."

"And what is our job in these talks to be?" The celebrity chef's assistant spoke up.

"Well, I'm sure you all recognize Chef Steward and Chef Slay. Together, they have the tricky task of coming up with a suitable dinner to host the talks between the aliens and the delegation sent from Earth's remaining governments. This will be no small undertaking! Kissinger hosted the Chinese diplomats in Hong Kong, not to the expected American-style cheeseburgers and fries, but to a fantastic, and painstakingly exact, Chinese meal. You chefs and your teams will be expected to do much the same, only using some of the aliens' delicacies."

Bethany, Bobby Slay's new sous-chef, spoke up. "What is this meal supposed to do? Do you really expect food to avert the aliens' attacks?"

"It is hoped that this meeting will be the start to that goal. If we can create some understanding between humanity and the Xanites, an end to the war might be possible. With a cease-fire, we could start to rebuild," the stressed official admitted.

"I used to work in the State Department, back when most of the government was still intact. I saw that, if the opposing sides could sit down long enough to enjoy some good food, surprising things could be accomplished. Our ultimate goal is to get them to realize that humanity is worth sparing. That's why this is so critical. If we can reach some common ground with them, we might just save civilization."

"I can get on board with that," Orlando, Marta Steward's sous-chef said. "Food is basic to most species that I'm familiar with, but did you really mean we have to cook an alien meal?"

The former State Department official ran his fingers through his hair. "There isn't enough information or time to do that. We've only been given a couple things to work with. I figure it's kind of a test, to judge the level of expertise and sophistication we can display. I have no idea what these items are or how to use them. That's where you all come in."

Someone in the audience piped up with, "But what if we accidentally make them sick?"

The official answered, "I can tell you that the items have been checked, and nothing is poisonous to either the aliens or humans. There should be enough to do a practice run and the final presentation. By the way, most human food is not hazardous to the aliens, if that helps. The only thing they might have a problem with is potatoes, so don't use those."

Bobby Slay spoke up. "I'm used to using strange and unfamiliar items in competition. If we have to do something with their products, there's no reason why they can't try some of ours, as well. We can show them how unique and stylish our food can be. I'm thinking that making some fusion cuisine might not be out of the question." He looked around to the others on his team, and they all nodded in agreement.

The government official, looking a little more confident, actually smiled. "It sounds like you're getting some ideas. Good luck to all of you, then. The fate of the world depends upon how well this goes!"

***

Marta Steward ushered her team into one of the kitchens previously designed to feed the hungry soldiers who worked on the clandestine base. The complex had actually been built with two kitchens, and both had been prepared and provisioned for the chefs to use.

"Let that young guy do the fusion stuff! Let's see what we have to work with here." She looked around the conventionally stocked kitchen. Gazing at the jar of powder sitting on the counter, she read the description. "Zaflortz, which is a phonetic approximation of what the aliens call this." Rubbing it through her fingers, she noted the flour-like texture. Inspiration came to her. "Team, take a little bit of this and we'll make a quarter-batch of biscuits. Let's see how that works."

The team lost their nervousness and settled into the familiar routine of baking.

***

Bethany accompanied the famous chef, Bobby Slay, into the other kitchen which had been prepared for their team. Chef Slay and his sous both walked over to the shiny stainless steel counter, on which sat a clear container of something which looked slightly opaque, viscous, and disgusting. The chef read the piece of paper out loud. "This is called flebosidy. Apparently much prized by the aliens." The contents coated the side of the jar as he twirled it around.

"More like phlegm, if you ask me!" the young woman joked.

He opened the lid and leaned in to smell the substance. "Hmm. No aroma."

Bethany watched with distaste. "You're not really going to…"

The intrepid chef had already dipped a spoon into the thick substance and brought it up to his mouth.

Thinking for a moment, Slay pondered the taste of the goop. "You know, this is much like a thickening agent. Similar to flour used in a roux. Actually, more like cornstarch, without any flavoring or spices added. It needs something."

The chef was at a loss. His greatest joy had been cooking with the freshest ingredients, but those were now in short supply. Looking around the kitchen, he thought furiously. "Bethany, what do we have to work with here?"

Bethany immediately went to the cupboards. "We have the fresh vegetables I've brought you. I also see an array of canned goods they've provided for our use," she informed him.

His sous moved to the refrigerator to tell the chef what was there. "Here, I see some fish, Chef. Looks to be river trout," she glanced at him hopefully.

Slay was doubtful that would help them. "The flavor would be too mild for a sauce as thick as this stuff would probably produce. What else is there?"

Stepping further into the walk-in refrigerator, Bethany came up with some hard-to-find hamburger. "What about this? Fatty, deeper flavor; ground beef might work with your proposed sauce."

The chef thought about her recommendation for a moment. "I like the idea of the deeper flavor, but hamburger might be a little too ordinary. Is there something else, maybe some other cut of beef in there?"

"Yes, Chef. There's not a lot to choose from, but I see there is a small beef roast in here. This cut won't have as much fat as the ground meat."

"I know, but it'll have to do," the chef said, considering his options. "Did you notice some bacon in the refrigerator? Something like that will add the fat. How about those fresh vegetables you were able to get? Any aromatics you can find in the pantry will give extra flavor. Just be sure to avoid the potatoes."

His sous dutifully came back carrying an armful of fairly fresh vegetables. He knew those were the best she could get under the circumstances. Turning to the rest of his team, he put them to work.

"Go get that cognac and burgundy. Let's get the onions and carrots rough-chopped and ready to go. Start sautéing the garlic and mushrooms with the bacon, too; that'll make this goop tasty and stretch the meat. We're going to make them the most remarkable and unique beef bourguignon they've ever tasted!"

"Yes, Chef!" his team, who had been listening, said in response.

***

Back at Marta Steward's kitchen, the trial run of biscuits was out of the oven and cooling. The famed cooking expert broke one apart to assess the results.

"The texture looks nice, and the rise is good. The aroma is a little more like almonds but the flavor isn't bad. Good job, team," she praised.

The rest of her staff tasted the results of their efforts and pronounced them appetizing. Her sous boldly spoke up, "If we're going to make biscuits, maybe we should add some cheddar cheese to the mix. It might up the flavor profile a bit. What do you think, Chef?"

"I like it. But double check to make sure the cheese won't cause problems. I don't want a diplomatic incident from something that came out of my kitchen!"

Orlando went to immediately discuss the food options with the former State Department official to make sure things would go smoothly.

Orlando gave Chef Steward the news that cheese would be safe. She thought further. "Biscuits might be a bit too homespun for a state dinner, though. Perhaps some cheese bread to go along with whatever Chef Slay is making, and then some cake for dessert? That should round things out. It's the best we can do. The aliens can't expect a multicourse feast after destroying most of our food production capability."

The remark about the destruction of so much of the continent's farm capacity caused a hard look from one of Marta's kitchen staff. When the rest got back to work, the savvy chef called her trusted aide over to her.

"Orlando, I want you to pay close attention to Pierre over there. I understand he harbors a grudge against the aliens. I just want to be sure he doesn't cause trouble."

"The poor guy lost his business, his home and his entire family in some of the worst of the alien attacks. I couldn't fault him for thoughts of revenge. Not one of us thinks of the Xanites as friends, but I understand that these talks are to end the killing and save what's left of our civilization. I agree with you that this is too important to have things go amiss. I'll watch him," Orlando sighed. He had plenty else to do besides keeping an employee out of trouble.

Pierre stepped into the pantry to get what he needed at his station. He was furious. "We're supposed to prepare food to save what's left of humanity? There isn't anything left. Most of humanity is dead. Their bodies were left to rot where they fell. My family has all died because of those worthless Xanites! The museums, the great architecture, the higher learning are all gone," he fumed to himself. "And we're hosting these killers? This idea that we might be able to placate them in the misguided hope they won't cause more destruction and death is ridiculous!"

In his anger, he dropped some eggs. As he bent to clean the mess up, a thought occurred to him. He slyly looked around to see if anybody else was paying attention, but the rest of the team was concentrating on their own duties. He knocked the rest of the eggs off the shelf.

Pierre went to Joseph, the person tasked with mixing the bread dough. Joseph had been industriously setting out what he needed for the task.

Pierre sidled up to the busy worker. "I'm afraid there's been an accident with the eggs. Someone spilled them all over the floor."

"I'll need an egg to spread over my bread before it bakes so the crust is shiny and golden. Now, I'll have to go to Chef Slay and see if they have any we can use. They won't be happy to hear about this." Joseph moaned.

"I'd go for you, Joe, but I don't want to give Chef Steward another reason to yell at me. You know how she is! But I'll tell you what I could do for you. To help, I'll get your bread dough started."

Joseph shrugged. "I can't see there'd be any harm in the help." He hurried over to the other kitchen to see if they could spare some eggs.

"Finally, I can strike back against the aliens," Pierre thought as he deliberately substituted potato flour to use with the zaflortz. "Eat that, you slime balls," he said under his breath.

Orlando came by at that moment and asked, "What was that?"

Pierre jumped. "Oh! I was just commenting that the dough will soon be ready to form a ball and be put to rise," he lied.

"Why are you working at this station?" Orlando queried. It hadn't escaped the sous-chef's notice that the man was acting in a guilty fashion.

Pierre went pale. "Well, there was an accident with the eggs. Joseph ran over to the other kitchen so nobody would notice. The guy's such a klutz, you know that. It's amazing he doesn't cause more accidents." He wiped his brow and hoped the sous didn't notice his invented tale.

Orlando just nodded, but he noted the furtive way Pierre was acting and his evasive responses.

***

In Slay's kitchen, the smell of beef simmering in a sauce of cognac and burgundy with garlic and onions was tantalizing. It reminded him of the "good old days" before the destruction the conflict with the Xanites had caused. He was deep in discussions with his staff when he was called over to talk to the negotiators of the Earth delegation.

"It certainly smells delicious," one of the representatives began cautiously. "However, we have some bad news for you."

"Oh? What's that," the chef asked, beginning to worry.

"Well, it seems the alien representatives are going to be early. They should be arriving in about half an hour from now," the lead negotiator stated.

"I need more time for the bourguignon. Wait! I have an idea. Have you told Chef Marta about the change yet?"

"We were just going over there." The delegation leader replied, his concern obvious.

Chef Slay thought fast. "When you talk to Chef Marta, perhaps you could suggest that the delegates might like some of her crackers. They're one of her specialties. She can put some cheese on them. I can provide cognac and burgundy. It's not much, but it'll do. The appetizers and drinks, with conversation, should stall them till my team and I are ready."

***

Orlando took a deep breath. The aromatic smell of warm, yeasty cheese bread reminded him that it had been a while since he'd eaten, and he was hungry. He noted that Marta was talking with the Earth diplomats. Her face had become red and she appeared angry. He wandered over to her side to lend assistance.

"Do you mean to tell me the aliens just decided to show up early?" the famous kitchen diva said in a deceptively low, yet menacing, voice.

"That is apparently so." The delegates looked decidedly uncomfortable under her glare.

Orlando spoke up to try to defuse the tension. "It may be another test. So what? The bread is done; the cake is cooling. We're almost ready to serve, right now."

The lead negotiator gave a smile. "Chef Slay's dish still needs to cook a bit longer. We hoped that you could serve some of your famous crackers to fill in the time till everything is ready... maybe with some cheese?"

At her withering frown, the negotiator's aide spoke up. "Chef Slay suggested he could provide things to drink. He mentioned cognac."

"How much time do we have to kill?" Orlando asked.

"About half an hour at this point," was the envoy's reply. "Some appetizers would fill in the gap till Chef Slay is ready."

The sous-chef consulted his watch. "It's doable, if we get to it now. I'll handle it," he said, in an effort to soothe the disgruntled chef.

Orlando hurried over to the bench where Pierre had been mixing the bread dough. He grabbed the bag of flour, reflexively turning it around to see what kind it was. He stopped dead in his tracks. Potato flour.

Grabbing one of the staff, he ordered them to make crackers quickly. "Get help if you need to. I have to see Chef Marta. Now!" he said as he sped away.

The chef looked at her trusted assistant as he hurried up to her. Her smile faded as she began to comprehend his agitated state. "Orlando, whatever is the problem? You said we were almost ready."

"I didn't anticipate this." He shoved the bag of flour toward her, with the label visible, so she could understand the difficulty. "I never counted on Pierre's treachery. It's one thing to dislike the aliens. Even to hate them. Their arrogant attitude has begun to grate on my nerves, to be sure. But this! This is sentencing all of humanity to a miserable end! We don't have a lot of time, and we can no longer serve the bread."

Marta thought for just a minute. "Then, we have no choice but to make a quick bread. Perhaps cornbread?"

"I'm on it," Orlando said, taking a breath to calm himself. He interrupted the person that was slicing the tainted loaf. "Leave that; it can't be served. Quickly, get me some onions or green onions, whichever are available. Get some from Chef Slay's kitchen if you have to."

The startled worker hurried to comply.

The concerned second-in-command pointed at another worker and said, "Get some cheese grated. Oh, and round up some cornmeal. If you can find jalapeños, bring those. We've got to make something quick. If we can do it, cornbread might just save this dinner."

Orlando worked with practiced speed to mix the cornmeal, cheese and remaining zaflortz with the other ingredients. That way, he could be assured nothing else would go wrong.

Pierre began to look around, unsuccessfully masking his guilt. As he was watching Orlando work with some staff to get the cornbread into the oven, he slowly crept closer to see what was going on. Unfortunately for him, Chef Marta was right behind him.

"Is something troubling you, Pierre? You're looking a little uncomfortable there, especially since everything was supposed to be almost ready for serving." She eyed him and continued, "You wouldn't happen to know anything about some sabotage, would you?" She just looked at him with her withering glare.

"I didn't do anything," he said, but his unconvincing lie sounded false. He couldn't make eye contact with the chef. His reaction told her everything she needed to know. She sensed immediately that he was guilty.

"What do you want me to do?" he whined.

"Here's what I'm ordering you to do: GET OUT OF MY KITCHEN!" Her bark had the desired effect.

The intimidated kitchen worker nearly stumbled as he quickly turned to leave. He stopped suddenly and turned around. His face was an irritated red and his eyes were on fire with fury. He angrily yelled, "So what if I used some potato flour when I wasn't supposed to? Who cares if it sickens or kills a few stinking aliens, anyway? Do you know what they did to my family? What they've done to most people's loved ones? What about your own families and friends? There isn't a person here who hasn't lost someone!"

The man continued his rant, sobbing. "They've wrecked my livelihood. Other people's as well. Those devils have destroyed our entire world! My life is ruined. There's nothing left for me! The economy has tanked and jobs are scarce. In firing me, you're helping them! Doesn't humanity mean anything to you? Why aren't you all fighting back?"

He quieted, looking around to the kitchen staff for some support. Some of the crew looked at him with sadness, though most avoided his gaze.

Marta fearlessly walked up to him and said quietly, "Does it help humanity one bit to kill the aliens who just might be willing to talk peace with us? All you're doing is prolonging the destruction till there's nothing left of humankind!"

"There's not much left of us now! How can you punish me for attacking them?" he yelled at her petulantly.

The woman wisely told him, "The difference is a shred of the knowledge we used to have still lives with those of us who are left. We survivors can pass that remaining understanding on to the next generation. The more experience we can convey means there is still a hope that civilization can be rebuilt." She continued in a solemn tone, "Your way is the end of everything that we ever knew and loved and aspired to achieve."

He slunk out, knowing that his life was going to get much worse before it got better, if it ever did.

***

The gangly-looking aliens arrived, only slightly earlier than expected. No known reports existed of any living humans who had encountered their species up close. Their deep-sea look was strange and unsettling.

"I'm glad I didn't go with the fish," Chef Slay said quietly to Chef Steward. The two stood together behind the scenes, watching the food being served.

"Chef Murimoto can do seafood better than you, anyway," Steward bantered back.

The younger culinary superstar just gave her a cocky grin. "Not when I give it my spicy flair!"

Anxiously, the two chefs turned their attention to the diplomats. They wanted to witness if their dishes would pass the culinary judgment of the aliens.

The predinner drinks had gone over well. Chef Marta's famous crackers were a hit with the humans and Xanites alike. The subtle almondlike flavor of the zaflortz was highly appreciated.

Both chefs watched as their main offerings were brought out to the table. Chef Slay grew nostalgic. "In televised competitions, each chef's dishes would be brought out individually. Here, the bourguignon and cornbread are being brought out together as a shared contribution of togetherness and hope."

"I like that," Chef Marta smiled, approving of the sentiment.

The food was served with stately aplomb. Alongside those dishes was a generous helping of butter for the cornbread. A dish of mixed vegetables was also provided. Nobody could say where the fancy china dishes, suitable for a diplomatic dinner, were obtained.

"The smells remind me of a time when fresh ingredients were taken for granted and more could have been offered. Now, such fresh food is an unexpected luxury," Chef Slay sighed. It was late in the season. Many farmers had been killed, and those who had survived weren't able to harvest much in all the unrest.

Marta nodded. "Some of what had once been productive farmland is now contaminated. The rest is too torn up. A new generation of farmers will have to learn to tend the fields to be able to grow anything. It'll take a long time before the land is fruitful again." She eyed her cake. It was a wonder to behold, with frosting on top. The dessert was a decadent indulgence in these lean times. The masterpiece was placed to the side, to be served after the guests had eaten dinner. She could only hope her offering would be appreciated.

The two chefs stood there, scrutinizing the guests. They could easily read the humans' expressions. "It looks like a good response from the Earth delegation. The aliens are harder to interpret," Marta noted. She watched as the tallest alien, who seemed to be the chief diplomat of the group, motioned both the chefs over to speak to them.

The being placed a translation device on the table, close to them, so the chefs could hear and respond. "This is an interesting dish," he or she indicated Slay's bourguignon. "I detect some flebosidy in it, but it is so much more flavorful than what we are used to. How did you do that?"

The famous chef was pleased. "It has onions and carrots in the sauce. They helped to add flavor. The flebosidy was used just to thicken it. Most of the flavor comes from the beef juices cooked with burgundy and cognac."

The ambassador considered that for a minute, then asked another question. "And what is this yellow substance that we were told to spread over the… cornbread, was it?"

Marta smiled and answered, "That's butter. It comes from cows, and there's nothing better on cornbread!"

The alien agreed, but seemed to look even more thoughtful. "In the – cornbread – there is something of a deeper yellow that is smooth and quite pleasing to taste. What is that?"

A little more hesitantly, Marta said, "That is cheese. It also comes from cows. I hope you found it to your liking."

"It was, indeed." The alien turned back to Slay and asked, "Tell me about this beef juice you mentioned. Where does that come from?"

It was Slay's turn to be a little flummoxed. "It comes from cows, too. The meat is from the animal, and the juice comes from the meat as it's cooked. Why? Is there a problem? We were told that you could handle our foods, except for potatoes. I assure you, there are no potatoes in any of these dishes!"

The lead diplomat looked troubled, and it was scaring the Earth delegates.

"Please allow me a few minutes to consult with my colleagues," the alien said, and leaned over to speak quietly with his aides.

The chefs moved away politely.

During the conversation, the translator that had been placed near the chefs had been left on. Whether that was to show no deception, or due to forgetfulness, nobody in the Earth delegation could determine.

"Show me a picture of a cow," the ambassador ordered one aide. He looked stricken when the picture was displayed and the device handed over to him. The associate seemed to be getting as uncomfortable as the Earth envoy was becoming.

The lead Xanite ordered his assistant to hand him a communications device. At that point, the Earth representatives were sweating profusely.

The translation equipment kept on working. The rest of the people at the table were all staring wide-eyed at each other, in the fear that some serious breach of diplomatic protocol had been committed.

The ambassador got through to a distant crew member. "Tell my brother and his friends that they are to immediately cease playing with the cows. What are cows? They are big, they have horns and… just tell those idiots to stop what they are doing with ALL Earth creatures! Yes, effective immediately. Do not argue with me; just do what I tell you! As of right now, cows are designated as valuable resources and are to be left alone. That is a standing directive. If I know my brother, he and his friends are probably out tormenting cows right now. I want you to go tell them to cease. And make some space in the supply area. I intend to have a large quantity of cheese and other things shipped home. What is cheese? Totally indescribable. Just wait till you taste it! The people on the home world are going to flip!"

The ambassador composed himself and turned back to the two chefs. "You both, and your teams, have shown a unique talent to join our foods with your own and create something totally new and delightful. I believe you call that fusion cuisine, do you not?"

The kitchen superstars could only nod silently in bewilderment.

"That displays a high level of mastery and sophistication. Linking our two cuisines indicates to me that perhaps our two cultures can also get along."

The ambassador looked down and grew thoughtful. "As a matter of fact, I was once allowed to leave after humans disabled my vehicle. They could have pursued me, but they did not. I survived, where I might have been easily killed. After that show of compassion and understanding, I worked to convince my government to cease the attacks. I believe that there is much to be optimistic about for our two species."

The two chefs' hopes were raised as the lead emissary continued. "We value those qualities of complexity and refinement. We also prize the innovation and creativity necessary to deal with the unfamiliar ingredients we tasked you with using. We gave you a short amount of time, but you showed an exceptional ability for adaptation. You both are to be commended."

The alien then addressed the entire group assembled at the dining table. "We have learned of the merits of the animals called cows. Creatures that can provide cheese and butter and beef juice are a valuable resource. On our world, it is against the law to squander such important assets."

The Earth delegation, hearing the Xanite's pronouncement, looked at each other with some relief.

"To that end, we are willing to discuss a cease fire if we can negotiate the importation of these Earth delicacies to our world," the lead envoy concluded.

Now the Earth diplomats were on familiar ground. The main human delegate stepped into the discussion. "Certainly, Mr. Ambassador, but our production capabilities have been severely curtailed. Much of our countryside and crops have been destroyed in the war. The very farmland that supports the cows you value so much has been devastated and many animals were killed. However, we could probably begin production to accommodate a limited amount of shipping as soon as our farms are repaired and running again."

"Nice way to suggest giving us some aid to get us back on our feet," Slay said appreciatively.

"Also a clever way to create a galactic market," Steward added. She, too, had been listening with anticipation. "You know, Slay, this is so much more than winning some base metal chef title. This is world class! Beyond that, this is truly a galaxy-level accomplishment! Instead of something that rusts, you'd be a… Molybdenum Chef!"

"Well, well, is that actually a compliment?" Slay grinned at his competitor who had turned into a culinary partner.

"Just don't let it go to your head," she couldn't help poking at the sometimes cocky superstar. "Remember, in reality, all we made was stew and cornbread. I hope I'm not going to become known for something that simple and mundane. Galactic comfort food, indeed!" she sniffed derisively.

"Hey, I'll take it, as long as it works," Slay decided. As the two chefs high-fived each other, they had renewed hope for the future.

Bittersweet

"Goodnight, Daddy."

"Goodnight, Sophie," Pierre whispered to his daughter as he covered her with the frilly unicorn comforter that was her favorite. "You are the cup of sugar in the recipe of my life!"

"Oh, Daddy!" Sophie gave a happy little-child giggle, which was why Pierre always said that to her before kissing her goodnight.

The sweetness of Pierre's dream vanished. He writhed in his sleep as the vision of the adorable little girl, safe and sound in her bed, morphed into Xanite attacks. The aliens had shown up and decided the Earth had resources they wanted.

In his nightmare, Pierre relived how he, his wife and child, and others who used to live in his neighborhood, had struggled to find some shelter after their homes were destroyed. "Let's try this shed," he suggested to his wife. They approached, but were warned off by a shotgun barrel poking out from the gap in the door.

They wandered around in the cold. "Finally, here's something at least," Pierre said. What they'd found was a little structure. It may have been a small shed, or even a shelter for a large dog. It was already occupied by another couple and their child, but Pierre's family was welcomed. "At least we'll be warm," he told them all gratefully. They huddled together in the dark.

"Be brave and try to be quiet," Pierre whispered to his frightened child as echoes of laser-fire and the pounding of space-launched attacks drew ever closer to where they cowered together.

The horrifying visions became even darker as his dream progressed. More attacks occurred. The sound still haunted him. At one point, the poundings eased. He had traveled out away from the shelter to try to find something, anything, for them to eat.

Pierre discovered some fiddlehead ferns and some mushrooms. He knew he needed to carefully check them in better light to be sure the mushrooms weren't poisonous, so he stuffed what he had found in separate pockets.

The alien bombardment started in again. He heard the sounds of the attacks increase in intensity and get closer. He ran back to his family with the food he had found, though in the dream he barely moved. The alien bombardment took out the little bit of shelter he and his family had found for the night. The sound was louder than anything else – it reverberated in his chest wall and hurt his ears. Then there was the deafening boom, and dirt and wreckage flew everywhere. The pressure wave briefly knocked him out. He didn't make it in time. In dream after dream, he never did.

As the dream progressed, he clawed through the wreckage where his family had been hiding only to find rubble. There was nothing left of his family and the other refugees. They were buried in the debris – no survivors.

Something had snapped in him then. The visions of destruction remained with him. The sight of the crushed, mangled bodies of his wife and child, curled up together, was indelibly inscribed in his memory.

With a cry, he sat up in his bed. A little blue nightlight showed him he was in his room at the communal housing area. Here, he had a room to himself. "At least this isn't the cramped relocation center," he sighed. There, he'd had only a cot in a large room filled with other cots, all occupied by people who were as devoid of hope as he was.

Before the alien attack, Pierre had trained to be a chef. "To think that once I even aspired to open my own restaurant," he sometimes fumed inwardly. That opportunity might have occurred when he got enough experience, if it hadn't been for the Xanites. Since then, his chances were as shattered as many of the derelict buildings.

To accommodate the number of displaced people, those who were fortunate lived in single rooms too small to include stoves. Therefore, food was prepared in communal kitchens for the hungry masses.

The people at the relocation center had found him another cooking job. It wasn't high-end. This place was more like a soup kitchen – but he knew he was lucky, since numerous survivors had skills that were no longer applicable. Dog catchers and data entry people weren't in big demand. Most of the banks were destroyed, and people mainly did business through barter, so accountants were unnecessary. Those left alive scrambled to adapt to this new situation.

With his new job, Pierre was able to afford this modest room, at least, but the joy had vanished from his life. In its place was just emptiness – a pit that could only be filled with revenge.

The sky was still dark, and so was his mood. "I might as well get up. I certainly won't get back to sleep." He threw his blanket off and got dressed.

This morning, it was his turn to try to acquire whatever vegetables and things could be found for the day's soup. He grabbed vouchers and carefully put a few in an interior pocket of his jacket. The rest he hid closer to his body to foil thieves.

A voucher took the place of money, allowing the person presenting it to have a bowl of soup, or it could be traded for something else. It was a makeshift way of paying the people who provided the food or services the kitchen needed.

Leaving the drab rooming house where he lived, Pierre tried to ignore the other people he passed. He kept his head down as he went on his way to the square where the locals sold their goods. In front of yet another decrepit-looking building, he tried to sidestep something nasty on the sidewalk. In doing that, he failed to notice someone lurking in the alley between the buildings.

"Hey!" Pierre yelled to the man as he was yanked into the shadows. The attacker tried to pull off the cook's jacket. "You must really be desperate to take my dirty old jacket, guy. It's not even that warm!" Pierre couldn't help but complain.

The mugger stank of sweat and desperation. He pushed Pierre down into the ooze and hit him. With the cook stunned, the attacker rummaged through the victim's pockets, finding the few vouchers that had been left in a more conspicuous place. The thief quickly ran away with as many as he could grab.

The poor cook was sore and momentarily helpless to stop the theft. "At least I only put a few in my coat pocket," he said as he collected himself. He was hurting from being struck, but he was dispirited at how far civilization had sunk. "Things weren't nearly as bad before those Xanites attacked. Can't somebody do something?"

Pierre tried to stand, but was still a little wobbly. Someone offered him a hand. "Looks like you could use some help. Here, let me." The stranger was burly. "My name is Jorland, by the way." His large hand was strong, and helped Pierre to get to his feet.

"I couldn't help overhearing your comment about changing things," the muscular man began. "If you really want something done, you've got to do it yourself."

"Why do I have to be the one?" Pierre groused, still a little woozy after the attack.

"Look around you," Jorland said. "Do you see anybody who is in a better position? Everybody, and I mean everybody, is beaten down. Most people are so used to it, they don't even remember a time when all this wasn't the case." The man gestured around to include all the filth and destruction.

"I can see you're old enough to have lived back when things were better. Fewer and fewer people who can remember are still alive to tell about it. Most of the survivors have only known this – the ruin that you see around you. To them, this is normal. It's the way things have always been."

Jorland reached into a pocket. "If you want to make things better, you'll have to decide to take some action. Here are directions to a spot where we're meeting tomorrow. Come, if you really want things to be different."

"Who's 'we'?" Pierre asked as he reached out to take the paper.

"Just a few like-minded people. Come alone. Bring that paper with you," the stranger warned and quickly left.

As he gathered himself together, Pierre thought about that encounter. "I don't know what I should do, if anything." He pondered the consequences of doing something versus doing nothing.

"Other than knowing how things were before the fall of society, what do I have to tell anyone?" That question stayed with him. "What do I remember, anyway? I could use an aspirin right about now, but they're in short supply. I recall that there used to be a police force that you could report a mugging to, and there used to be emergency medical services that you could call to get help. I really miss being able to phone for pizza or e-mail a friend." His thoughts went round and round.

***

The morning's provisions were meager due to the stolen vouchers, but Pierre was able to forage in the woods surrounding the settlement for some mushrooms and ferns. He even found a rabbit in a snare someone hadn't collected yet. "At least there will be a little meat in the stew today," he said, only slightly appeased by the supplemental fare he was providing.

He informed his coworker, Joseph, about the theft of some of the vouchers. The two set to work chopping the vegetables and dealing with the meat. "At least with this rabbit, you won't be in too much trouble for losing the vouchers," Joe said.

Joseph was a decent guy who had tried his best to make the disagreeable, moody Pierre feel more at home with the rest of the kitchen workers. He'd empathized when Pierre had gotten fired from his previous employment. "It was a good job, but unfortunately he got in trouble for some things he'd done. He's had a rough time of it. You'd be angry, too, if you'd lost your family and your job and any prospects, one right after the other," Joe had explained to the others.

Pierre wanted to try to respond to the man's kindness, but was rusty at it. He eventually stated the major thing that had been bothering him this morning. "The vouchers don't go as far as they used to. Everybody has increased their rates."

Joe just shrugged his shoulders. "That's to be expected. Everyone is trying to put away food for their own use, now that the growing season is pretty much over. With winter near, they'll also probably save a few of the vouchers they've received so they can get a bowl of hot soup when they've used up most of their private supplies."

Pierre could understand that. "Winters seem to be lasting longer and getting colder. Have you noticed that?"

"I've noticed," Joe said sadly. "It's mostly due to the particulates in the air from all the attacks. I'm afraid that if things get worse, there won't be a long enough growing season. Mass starvation will set in. People get dangerous when they're hungry. That'll make things a lot worse."

"Aren't things already pretty desperate?" Pierre couldn't help asking, his own anger and bitterness seeping into the question.

"Well, not like the situation could get. The big cities don't have the farm resources close at hand, like we have here. As things got worse, deliveries of food and necessities stopped happening. I've heard talk that people there ransacked buildings and stole what they could. The younger folks were quicker to adapt to the gang mentality and follow along. Those who tried to resist were shot."

"What about the older people?" Pierre was almost afraid of finding out.

"They were slower and weaker. Because they couldn't provide muscle, they were considered useless. Those few who could escape told of people in power killing the old and infirm ones and taking their food and useful belongings like spoils of war. Imagine activity like that happening here." Joe shook his head sadly.

The kitchen worker continued, "You know, I vaguely remember something about a past conflict. When one group took over, they left the younger people, but killed the older ones, all because the parents and grandparents could remember when things were different."

That sparked a thought of what Jorland had said. Pierre turned, suddenly needing to ask the question: "Do you really think that telling the younger survivors about the way things used to be would make a lot of difference to them?"

Joe stopped what he was doing for a heartbeat. "That depends, I guess. We're all just struggling to make it through another winter. Some might take that information and see possibilities for improving our situation. Others, though, might just see it as something to envy or ridicule. I could see that jealous faction asking, 'If things were that good, why couldn't you have resisted the invaders?'"

Pierre didn't have an answer to that. He thought for a moment. "So, it sounds like maybe the younger children might be more able to use the concepts anyone might pass on, but the rest are too busy surviving?"

"The rest are too beaten down to care one way or the other. Science and mathematics don't matter much to you when you're just trying to live another day."

"So, first building a safer, more secure environment would allow for more learning?" Pierre surmised.

"I suppose. Say, what's got you so fired up all of a sudden?" Joe looked questioningly at his usually withdrawn buddy.

Pierre didn't want to talk about the secret meeting. He was afraid it might be a bad thing for both himself and his friend.

"I guess the run-in with that thief shook me up more than I realized," he offered as an explanation.

***

The evening of the clandestine meeting, Pierre finally made up his mind. He just barely made it to the grove of trees on time. Hurrying left him out of breath, and he was already anxious from fear and anticipation.

"Hello," he hesitantly called out once well inside the woods. For a while, there was no sound. Suddenly, someone stepped out in front of him. It was just a scrawny boy, probably not much older than his early teens.

"What're you here for?" the teen demanded.

"I'm here for a meeting. Why do you need to know?" Pierre shot back at the unhelpful kid.

"Who are you meeting?" the adolescent challenged.

Pierre was silent as he tried to remember the name the stranger had given him. "Jorgen? No, Jorland. That's the guy I'm here to meet. Why isn't he here?"

"Show me the paper," the youth commanded, and looked it over carefully. The teen seemed satisfied and stuffed it in a pocket. "He sent me to meet you and take you the rest of the way. If you hadn't come alone, like he said, I would have ignored you."

"What if I hadn't shown you that paper?" Pierre nervously asked.

"We wouldn't be having this conversation," was the terse reply. The teen moved his coat slightly at his hip to display a gun.

"All right, now what?" Pierre was getting tired of this conversation, which was getting nowhere.

"Just follow me. Try to keep up, old timer."

The teen obviously knew where he was going and was nimble enough to go through the woods at a fast clip. Pierre was hard-pressed to keep up. "Old timer," the cook muttered, as much annoyed at himself as at the fast-moving youngster.

When they finally left the forest, Pierre was led to a building in a valley.

"No wonder I didn't know about this. It couldn't be seen from the town's side of the woods," Pierre wheezed. He was forced to stop and catch his breath. "How did you meet these people?

"Quiet," the adolescent warned. He stopped to remember, then continued in a whisper. "Well, I was cold and hungry. I was also very angry when my family was killed. They gave me food and a purpose when I needed it."

"Yeah, I could use a better purpose for my life, too," the cook said honestly, pondering the comparisons with his own life experiences.

The teen nodded in silent understanding. "Wait here," he finally said, and left.

Soon a door opened in the building, displaying strong white light from within. "That's too bright to be candlelight. They must have power," the cook briefly thought.

Jorland came out and greeted him. "Forgive me, but I need to make sure you don't have any weapons," the big man stated casually. He ran something along Pierre's body, from side to side.

"Hey, I've seen those metal detectors before," Pierre said.

"And that's why those who have enough life experience need to pass it on. The teens, one of whom you've met, still get nervous around this technology. With no background in science and engineering, it's beyond them how electronic equipment functions. To them, it becomes nearly magical stuff. Follow me and let's get inside."

Indoors, Pierre was greeted by the rest of the group, most of whom he didn't recognize. Nobody asked his name, but they were friendly. Jorland told him, "Names are not important at this point."

They were mostly adults, like Pierre. A few teens were there, standing by the walls, listening.

Jorland began to speak to everyone. "Let's get right to it. What's the biggest problem you have right now? In a word, it's starvation. The weather is cooling and the growing season is shortening. I have something that I think will help you." He brought out a barrel of something that Pierre couldn't see.

One of the old men took a look inside it and smiled. "I recognize that! I haven't seen it in many years, but when I was a youngster farming with my dad, we'd plant winter wheat like that. It was about this time of year, too. We didn't have to spend effort on plowing the existing stubble. We just seeded the winter wheat into the ground in the fall. It survived the cold and we could harvest it in early spring."

Jorland was pleased that the old man understood what he was trying to do. "This year's harvest might get you all through this winter. However, food is steadily becoming scarce, and it's expected that this haze may last a couple years or more. This type of wheat can survive the cold that we're experiencing, so these seeds will help you get through the lean times that are sure to come. Plant these and take some of the crop to grind for flour to use in bread. If you keep aside some of the seeds you've reaped, you can use them for planting next fall. That way you have some food to eat to survive next winter. Keep saving seed for next time, and you can survive winters after that, too."

"This is an awful lot of seed for just our little community," an ill-tempered older man groused. "What're we supposed to do with all that wheat, come harvest time?"

"Just like I said," Jorland answered, "Save some seed for next year. If you have more than you can use after harvesting and processing, cooperate with neighboring communities and share resources. That's how this will work. You help them and they'll help you. Then they do that with their neighbors and the benefit spreads. Together, you can steadily make the situation better for everyone."

Time passed, and nobody spoke up. They all took a moment to mull over what they'd heard. Pierre had a thought. "Will this really make that big a difference?"

"All I can say is, I hope so. It won't be overnight. If everybody shares, everybody has enough to eat. When survival is more assured, then people can move on to things like education and rebuilding." Jorland looked from Pierre to the others, with sincerity in his eyes.

"So, what's in it for you?" The testy oldster insisted.

"Hopefully, I get to live to see civilization reemerge." Jorland looked at them all with a serious gaze. "If not, we all die. No more civilization. No more people."

The talk of progressing from survival to relearning skills sparked something in Pierre, and he suddenly had an urge to contribute. It was something he hadn't felt for a long, long time. "You know, if somebody can grind the grain into flour, I can make it into bread. The kitchen where I work has ovens, but they're rarely used because of energy concerns. These days, the kitchen serves soup. It doesn't take as much energy to build a fire to heat water. Bread would work well with the soup to fill people's stomachs."

A woman Pierre had seen around town suddenly smiled and spoke up. "I know a family further out from the town. They just grind what they use, but if they could grind grain for the town as well, and this man could make the bread, we're getting started on surviving a long winter!"

Even the grouchy old man from before began to pick up the other people's enthusiasm. "I suppose I could lend a generator to run the ovens. I'd expect to be compensated, though!"

A third person timidly spoke up. "If I can convince them, I might be able to find a source for butter and milk and cheese. Would that help?"

The enigmatic Jorland spoke up; "I'll let you all deal with the details and work things out." He turned to leave, but Pierre could have sworn he heard the big man say, "And this is how it starts!"

People were too busy getting together in clusters to notice that Jorland had quietly left. One group discussed the planting of the seed. Another bunch hashed out the grinding and distribution of the flour. Other people talked about how to get the ovens working.

As Pierre added to the discussion here and there, he had a spark of hope. With years of sadness and anger, his face had creased in a perpetually sour expression. Now, he was actually smiling, and the happiness he felt showed itself in his eyes, as well.

The woman who had shyly spoken about a source for dairy products caught his eye. She smiled back at him. "So, do you really think you can make something with this flour? It won't be as fine as the manufactured stuff I remember."

His gaze took her in. She was old enough to remember "before," but still young enough to interest him. "Some rustic types of bread are supposed to be coarse and chewy. It may take a little trial and error, but I could do it," he said with confidence.

He was amazed at how easy it was to just open up after the grief of his losses. Thinking quickly, he actually added, "And any butter we could get would go well on crusty, warm bread! If you could convince that source of yours, I'd have to make you a special loaf myself!" He smiled, surprising himself by flirting a little with her. "And imagine some cheese rolls! Heavenly!" he enthused.

"You're making me hungry," she said. She suddenly blushed at the way her words could be taken.

"Everyone is, but this could help," Pierre said. He was careful to keep to her obvious meaning because he didn't want the attractive woman to shy away. "I used to be a trained chef. There once was a time when I could have made something fancier than soup. Even something as mundane as a frittata is next to impossible to make now, with the scarcity of ingredients."

"That's why I came tonight. I was afraid, but I felt I needed to see for myself what others might do and…" She looked up at him, her sudden flush of confidence fading.

"And, you wanted to see if you might have anything to contribute?" Pierre added for her. Her nod encouraged him. "It seems the meeting is breaking up. May I accompany you? At least, for as long as you're comfortable, so we can continue our conversation?"

At first she looked hesitant, but then she gave Pierre that smile that had captured his attention. "Well, at least till we get to the outskirts of town. Then I will have to turn off. It would be nice to have somebody with me through those woods, though." She shuddered a little.

Pierre offered her his hand. Once they got out of the building and were away from the others, he stopped. "I'm Pierre, by the way. I work at the soup kitchen, but I don't recall seeing you there."

"I mainly work on my family's farm. I don't make it into town often. I didn't feel like I should say something in the meeting, but we would be the ones who could provide the butter, milk and cheese. I'm Harmony. It's nice to meet you."

Pierre suddenly felt different. He bowed slightly in an old fashioned way to gently kiss her fingers.

She gasped a little, but he hoped it was in pleasure.

"I will be pleased to escort you, Harmony, for as long as you will allow me."

They both smiled. As they walked along, the couple spoke of many things. Memories from before the devastation and the deaths of those close to them were recounted.

"It seems we've both lost family. That is especially hard," Harmony said sympathetically. "I was engaged to someone, but he was killed by desperate people who stole what little he had." She looked down at the road and said no more for a while as they walked further.

Eventually, to fill in the silence, Pierre confided, "I lost my wife and child. I went crazy with grief and did some unbelievable things that still make me uncomfortable." The admission somehow made him feel lighter.

"Did you kill somebody?" The worry in Harmony's voice was evident, even if he couldn't see her face.

He quickly answered, "No. But I wanted to, believe me."

"Wanting to do it is something I can understand. But I'm glad you didn't." Her smile was visible as the clouds parted and the moonlight revealed her face.

When they got to the point where Harmony stopped to turn off for her parents' farm, Pierre told her, "This has truly been the best evening I've had in a very long time. I can't help wishing it didn't have to end. Is there some way we might see each other again?"

With a slight breath in, she hesitated. Then that smile got wider and she said, "Yes, I'd like that. I can find some reason to go into town sometime. I'll be sure to stop into the soup kitchen to see you." She turned down the path and soon disappeared around some bushes.

When she was lost from his view, Pierre thoughtfully continued home. Things felt different. He felt more alive. Entering his room, he noticed it didn't feel so bleak. Even his usual routine before bed didn't seem so pointless. He actually hummed a snippet of a song he couldn't remember the words to anymore.

***

The sound woke Pierre up. "What's that noise?" he grumbled. "Oh! It's my alarm. I haven't heard that in such a long time. Last evening was the first time I've slept completely through the night since the attacks."

He got to the soup kitchen a few minutes early and was eager to start. That hadn't happened before.

"Hey! You're looking chipper and you aren't late. What's up?" Joe teased him.

Pierre didn't laugh at the teasing, but he looked thoughtful. Instead of a gruff remark, he just responded, "You know, last night was the first time I didn't have nightmares."

"I could tell things have been rough on you for some time now. That's good that things are getting better. Why the change, though?" Joe queried.

Pierre silently turned to get to work on the day's soup, but thought of what had altered in his life. The difference was Harmony.

"The past is the past, but I'm beginning to think that maybe the future could be better than things are now. I just never saw that before," Pierre said.

His friend nodded in agreement.

The two cooks settled into a familiar routine of preparing the ingredients and making the day's soup.

Sometime after the midday meal rush was over, someone else came through the front door to the kitchen. The bells at the door tinkled lightly.

"Be out in a minute," Pierre called. "Sit anywhere at the counter and I'll get some soup for you."

A soft and familiar voice called out, "I'm not here for soup, although it smells delicious."

As soon as Pierre heard Harmony's voice, he got a big grin on his face and hurried out. "Hello," he said awkwardly. It took him a minute to figure out what else to say. "Are you sure you wouldn't like a little cup of soup, at least? The weather's pretty cold and it'll warm you up."

"No, but thank you," she said. "I have something for you. Do you think you can find a use for this?" She held out a cloth-covered object to him.

Opening it, Pierre saw a hunk of yellow cheese. "Oh!" he said appreciatively, smelling it. "Once the ovens are finally up and running, some of this is going into cheese rolls!" He smiled at her in enthusiasm.

"When will that be?" she asked.

"It should be by tomorrow, barring any problems," he smiled triumphantly. "I have some remaining flour which will last till this crop of winter wheat gets harvested and distributed. Once that happens, we'll really be up and running!"

"I love seeing you so optimistic," Harmony said, sharing his enthusiasm.

Pierre came around the counter and said, "Allow me to thank you properly." He gave her a quick kiss.

***

The winter came, and it was the coldest and longest Pierre and Harmony could recall. By then, the townspeople knew it was time to throw the couple a pairing party.

***

"I recall that, at first, my parents had to be convinced to trade milk, cheese and butter with you, but when they got a taste of your rustic breads, they knew you were on the right track with this!" Harmony praised, as Pierre brought a few more loaves out of the ovens.

"I remember that." He looked lovingly at her.

Harmony decided it was much more comfortable helping out in the back where she could sit down. Her girth had expanded with her pregnancy and she got tired sooner. Her pregnancy was one of the increasing births expected in the town.

A midwife actually moved into town to be close for the deliveries. "The town's population is growing and the things I need are close at hand," she said. The number of goods and services the town could offer to inhabitants had gotten bigger with the population.

Pierre was gratified to see that conditions in the town were slowly getting better. There was even a small police force. None of the officers had matching uniforms, but it was a start.

This year's spring was a weak shadow of what they remembered it to be. When summer finally came, it was cooler than people recalled, but it gave people confidence that the season would last a bit longer than it had in past years. The hope was that the particulates would continue clearing from the air.

"As more plant life comes back, the soup of the day becomes more varied and hearty, and the people have satisfying bread to go with it. It makes me feel good that I can have a hand in it," Pierre said to Harmony.

"I am so glad we seem to be nearing the end of all of this cold," she smiled back optimistically. As usual, she gave him a little kiss and continued about her kitchen duties.

The little bells tinkled at the door, and a scrawny youth walked in. It was Pete, one of the teens Pierre recognized.

"How are you doing, Pete?" Pierre asked jovially. "Need some soup? It still gets chilly out there."

Pierre dished up a hearty bowl, knowing the kid would work in the kitchen in return for it.

"How is your friend, Josh?" The cook asked sympathetically. Pierre knew Pete's friend was prone to mixing with the wrong crowd. "Is he staying out of trouble?"

"I don't see him much anymore. He got involved with some group. I don't remember their name. It was something like 'Human Sovereignty' or something. They're unhappy that the Xanites are trading with us now. He wanted me to join, but it didn't suit me." Pete stopped talking long enough to dig into the soup that had been placed in front of him.

The youngster's information worried Pierre. He knew how close he, himself, had come to wreaking carnage on somebody out of a need for revenge.

"That's not good news," the cook said sadly. "If you see him, you can tell him that I've got a job for him here, if he wants it. I can't pay much, but there's food. And if he just wants to talk, I'd be happy to listen."

The hungry teen nodded as he devoured the last of what was in his bowl and sopped up the remains with some bread.

Pierre grinned. It was satisfying to see the simple needs of life met and gratifying that he could help do so.

"Now that you're done, take your dish into the kitchen. Help Harmony by making sure there's some clean water brought in for tomorrow's soup." Pierre directed with a smile.

The cook soon returned to the kitchen and saw that Harmony was directing Pete on the next day's preparations. He smiled till he saw the pinched look on her face.

"Are you all right, my dear?" he asked. She smiled, but it was a pained one which didn't lessen his worries.

"Oh, I begin to think this child is impatient to be born. We're about at the end of the time when Dara figured the baby would come," she said. "The pains are coming so frequently, I can't concentrate on anything else."

She winced in discomfort at another contraction. He quickly told Pete to stop what he was doing. "Run and get Dara, the midwife. Tell her to meet us at home."

He bundled Harmony into her coat and helped her the few blocks to the room where they both lived. It didn't take long for Dara to show up. She and Pierre helped Harmony get more comfortable in preparation for giving birth.

***

"How much longer will it be?" Pierre asked the midwife again.

"Not too much longer now. I can see the baby's head."

Harmony cried out in pain, and Dara directed Pierre to wring out a cloth in a bowl of cold water and place it on her brow.

"Here it comes!" Dara suddenly said. In admiration, she continued, "She's a beautiful little girl! Do you have a name picked out?"

Pierre wiped his wife's brow and said, "Well, we tried out all sorts of names, but nothing seemed to really fit."

Once Dara placed their baby girl in Harmony's arms, Pierre looked at them and almost cried for joy. When his child was placed in his arms, his face lit up. Smiling at his tired wife, he said, "You and our daughter bring so much happiness to my life. Because of you, I've been filled with such harmony and hope!"

Harmony laughed a tired laugh. "And Hope sounds like it would be a fine name for this little one."

Pierre and Dara agreed.

Somewhere in the back of his head, Pierre heard a long forgotten voice of a big man who had helped him to dream of new possibilities. "And that's how it starts."

The Mask of the Seamstress

The sunlight was behind the trees and the shadows were descending upon the campground. The youngsters sitting around the campfire had all been trying to frighten each other with scary stories.

"Now it's my turn," Bob spoke up with childish enthusiasm. He was eager to outdo his friends.

The other children scooted nearer in anticipation as the darkness closed in on them. The dancing flames created eerie shadow movement around the area.

"Let's see. It seems there was this old woman who made masks for people. They all had to wear one to hide their hideous faces. The people sometimes decorated their masks, too." Bob was enjoying the attention he was getting from the other children. "My grandfather told me that people put funny sayings, or pictures, or stuff like that on their masks to keep from being afraid. He said it boosted people's morale. There is a story that this old seamstress made a mask for a bride. That covering had a mark on one side of it, like a smear of blood. Both the bride and groom died soon after it was worn. After that, no one dared to copy the design of the red drop."

The children became agitated in fear. Bob continued, enjoying the reaction. "On nights when it's dark and misty, if you're walking down a lonely road, it is said that you might see the shadow of the bride wearing that cursed mask. Some say that mark on the mask is visible even in the gloom. Some people think she's looking for her lost husband, while others say she's seeking to avenge her death. Since that time, it was whispered that if anybody ever wore a mask with a red drop on it, bad things would follow the wearer. All because of that doomed bride. If you see her, you'd better run away because it means you're going to die!"

The rest of the children gasped. They were definitely scared by the tale.

One brave child dared to ask, "I've never heard that story. Why haven't any of our parents warned us about this before?"

Bob got a wicked look in his eyes and leaned forward to his frightened companions. "My grandfather also said that bad things will *always* happen to those who talk about it. That's probably why you never heard this before. Nobody dares to tell the tale. If the mask does show up, nobody should take the risk of handling it, or they'll be cursed, too."

The children's eyes got big in fright. After a pause, one of the more thoughtful children spoke up, "Bob, how come *you* can tell the story?"

The clever young storyteller just smiled and said, "Nobody has to wear masks anymore, so we're all safe!"

The inquisitive child considered what he'd heard and didn't believe Bob's tale. "What kind of things did you say they put on their masks, if putting a teardrop on was bad?"

"My grandpa said they'd put things like 'Alien bioweapons suck' or things like that. He also said they used other words that I'm not allowed to say, but you get the idea!"

The children all looked at each other till one was curious enough to ask, "What are alien bioweapons?"

All the innocent eyes looked to the "campfire leader," as the adult was honorifically called, to answer the question.

"When the aliens first came, they were used to illnesses that humans hadn't ever encountered. Humans got sick, almost like the yearly round of influenza, until most people had developed a natural immunity to it. Mainly, it was like a bad stomach flu, which made a person upchuck and have to poop a lot. A few, however, didn't recover and died. Most were mainly just miserable for a while till they got better. On the other hand, a lot of the aliens were made sick from bacteria and viruses that humans had immunity to, and back and forth it went. So you see, the sickness wasn't an actual bioweapon, which is something that is created and specifically spread to cause terrible illness and death. It was just natural occurrences."

The leader tried to keep the story low-keyed and as non-graphic as possible. In his younger days, he'd been in the military. He'd seen plenty of death and carnage, so he was happy not to go into detail. At least his explanation seemed to satisfy the kids.

"That was a pretty good story, Bob. Somebody else, tell us a scarier one!" a youngster called out. All the children were eager to hear something else.

"Now, now," the adult watching over the bunch of kids cautioned. "Let's not get each other too scared. Frightening yourselves till you can't sleep through the night and aren't able to function the next day isn't the way to be ready for tomorrow's lessons! Your parents expect you to learn a little about how to survive in the wilderness."

"Why do we have to learn this foraging stuff, anyway? Couldn't we just go to the market and get food?"

The absolutely innocent and untroubled looks from all the students gathered around the fire touched the leader. Their reactions also informed him that these kids understood almost nothing about the devastation and deprivation their grandparents had lived through during the Xanite attacks.

"I understand that you're used to your parents getting food from the local markets. That may be a normal occurrence for you all, but it wasn't always so. There was a time when the sunlight couldn't get through the clouds. Now that the sun isn't obscured, the snow and the cold have subsided. The land is fertile and crops can be grown again."

Someone wanted to know, "Why was it cloudy all the time?"

The adult answered, "It was because of all the destruction. That left a lot of smoke in the air. The sky was cloudy and dark. There was less sun, so it was almost like winter most of the year. With the cold, food became scarce. Medicine and clothes were harder to get. People had to make do with whatever they could find. Some grew hardy plants that could survive, even in the cold. Still, there were too many people who starved and died. That's why you're being taught to find food in the forest. As you progress in your lessons, you'll learn about growing your own crops. You'll be shown what to plant in spring and what to sow in the fall." Bad memories of living through those harsh times began to flood the former Green Beret's mind.

The children didn't look like they understood.

"You won't starve if you know what plants are edible. There is plenty of food in the wild if you know where to look. I'll teach you so you know where to find it. Chickweed, field garlic and dandelion are all edible, and learning this means you will be self-sufficient. When you don't rely on others, you strengthen the entire group. After that, if you have a little extra food or goods, it's proper to share with the rest. When an emergency arises, if you can help provide for those who are in need, you'll be an asset to the community."

The children looked blankly at the campfire leader. "Mr. Jorland, can you tell us a story about those times?" They all looked pleadingly at him, and he found it hard to resist.

"Those days weren't fun. Nobody had an easy time getting through the devastation. The ones who survived had to be pretty tough and determined. That is why you are being taught some of the skills your grandparents had to pick up the hard way. They want things to be a little easier for all of you."

The old man tried to recall a story that could be used to teach the clueless kids without totally traumatizing them. While he searched his memory to pick an appropriate tale that would showcase various skills, he added another log to the fire. That gave him the time to make up his mind.

"Well, that story Bob over there told about the old seamstress isn't quite right. Let me tell you the real version. Because of the attacks, many cities were in ruin. Even if a factory survived, people were fleeing, so there was nobody to make anything, not even the masks."

"Bob's story talked about masks. Tell us why people wore them. We don't need them now," one child interrupted.

Jorland poked at the fire for a bit. "As you heard, the masks were needed to keep from breathing in all the dust and ash and bad stuff. They helped to protect people's lungs. There was sickness, too, so the masks were useful to keep people from getting ill. As I mentioned before, both the Xanite populations and the human ones had diseases which caused problems till the other side could develop immunity to it."

"People couldn't just go to the market and get coverings?" one innocent voice called out.

"No, they couldn't. Remember, the factories that made things like masks were destroyed. So, people began putting together face coverings for themselves. Some people could sew better than most, so they used that skill to make masks for others. In that way, they helped their entire communities. Like I've said before, when you use a skill you have for everyone's benefit, you help the entire group."

"You mean like Bob's story of the old woman?"

"Shhh," another child admonished.

The leader nodded. "Exactly. As I recall, she wasn't really that old, although a bit older than all of you. There was destruction all around. Some buildings had burned to the ground, while others left nothing but metal skeletons pointing up to the sky. The Xanites pounded many cities from ships way up high, and they also had machines that devastated the remaining populations on the ground."

One child was bold enough to speak out in doubt. "Is that what those rusting things are? Nobody can build anything that tall!"

"Yes, that's what those metal remnants are. Once, we really were able to construct buildings that high," the adult assured the unbelieving student. "You can see what's left of the structures for yourselves." He pointed to the rusting spires on the horizon. "Humanity could do other things, too. Maybe someday we'll be able to do those things again." The look of sadness on his face was noticed by the children.

"After the attacks, people had to resort to doing what they could by hand. This is the story of the mask maker, who did what she could for her community when they needed it," Jorland began.

Wood smoke permeated the camp site, adding to the ambiance of the story. The pop and hiss of the fire almost began to sound like distant gunfire and laser blasts.

***

The ground rumbled from the latest orbital pounding. The Xanite ground vehicles began getting nearer and nearer to their village. Gedney winced. "Those aliens are getting closer every day. If this continues, we could get bombed as well. All the outlying communities are reaching the point where they don't have enough room and resources to absorb any more refugees. Waves of people have to travel farther and farther to get away."

She paused, looking out her dusty window. Long lines of people walked dispiritedly down the streets, taking advantage of the easier travel. These little villages had, at one time, been called suburbs. What had once been well-tended lawns were now patches of gardens to grow food.

The remnants of the demolished city's displaced population clustered in these communities. Some came temporarily to regroup with family and friends who had gotten separated and move further along. Others would try to stay and rebuild their lives, hoping for sanctuary from the combat.

Trying to get further away took strength that not many of the malnourished refugees had. Beyond the scattered settlements, there was nothing but rough, overgrown areas or craters. Trekking across the fragments of roads destroyed by earlier bombardments, or through tangled acreage that had never been built up at all, was an unenviable task. It took determination and bravery to try.

Desperate strangers with nowhere else to go kept filing across Gedney's view, only to disappear into the murky overcast caused by the smoke and particulates from the recent bombings in the area. There was little talk, and no hope in their faces. They had no goal – they were just trying their best to flee yet another area of destruction.

"Isn't somebody supposed to be doing something?" The young woman was saddened to see so many anxious people and know there was little she could do to ease their suffering.

Her brother, Lucanin, spoke up, "Back when there was still some sort of command and control capability, there was a more coordinated effort to fight back against the aliens who were ravaging the land and stealing our resources. That leadership has been lost, and local areas are left to do what they can with what little they have on hand. The survivors are left to deal with the situation on their own. Communication and organization have broken down so extensively that there is no hope of a unified effort anymore. These people have no recourse but to try to resist if they can, or get out of the way as the wave of destruction moves from area to area."

Sadness beyond his years shaded his face. Too many unhappy memories came to mind. He decided not to dwell on them. "All we can do at this point is wait and see if the bombardment gets much closer. If it does, we may be forced to join the evacuation, too."

Gedney noticed that most of the people had tied scraps of fabric around their faces to try to filter the smoke and make breathing a little easier.

"Even though you were wounded in the conflict and can't move fast enough to fight any more, you do a good job tending to our little garden. You see to it that we have something to eat, and any extra food goes to help the community. Your idea to put scraps of clear plastic sheeting over the ground to help keep it warm and moist was brilliant! You're an asset to us all. I don't know what I'd do without you. I want to be helpful as well, but I just don't think I'd make a good fighter," she fretted.

Her brother tried to lend a positive outlook. "You provide an important service to the community by binding people's wounds. The sewing and mending you do is the best in the village. That's also a worthwhile contribution. I'm sure you can come up with any number of other things you could add to the group if you choose."

"I suppose you're right. I currently have a sewing project for a bride's wedding outfit. With all the continued bombings putting smoke and ash in the air, she's going to be coughing throughout the ceremony." Gedney stopped to think. "I see all the evacuees with makeshift masks over their noses and mouths. Since the bride's attire is pretty much done, what's left of the fabric for her dress will make a coordinating mask for her to wear on her wedding day! In fact, I could sew any leftover fabric remnants for people to use. That would certainly be helpful."

Lucanin nodded in agreement.

Gedney felt happy that she could provide something else to help the group. She set about making facial coverings. It took her a few tries to make it work, but she got into a rhythm and began to turn them out at a prodigious rate. Once she figured out how to do it, she used the fabric scraps from the bride's dress and some matching lace to fashion a pretty wedding mask.

She concentrated on the task and forgot about dinner. Lucanin had harvested a cabbage and a few carrots from the garden behind their modest house. He had put the vegetables in the broth for soup. About the time their meal was ready, there was a knock at their door.

A neighbor stopped by, his nose twitching at the flavorful smell. "I wanted to ask if you have anything to donate to the refugees. This group is pretty bad off. These people didn't have time to gather anything before being forced to flee."

Lucanin grimaced at the thought. "The first ones who traveled past here started off by trying to take everything they could haul or drag with them. A lot of their possessions got dumped by the roadside because the things were too hard to carry and not useful. Later groups took only the necessities they could easily pack. Things are getting worse when people have to run with only the clothes on their backs and whatever is in their pockets." He exhaled sadly. "All we have is this pot of soup. It isn't much, but it's at least something. If they're hungry, they'll eat it, even though it isn't fancy."

Pouring two bowls, one for himself and the other for his sister, Lucanin gave the remainder to the neighbor to distribute. "Here you go, Sam. I'll need the pot back, please," he told the helpful townsman, who nodded and gratefully took the container of soup.

Before Sam could leave, Gedney said, "I'm making some masks for the ones who could use them. A bunch of them are ready. If you send someone, they can take this box to distribute among the refugees. I hope it'll do some good."

"That is the nicest thing I've heard of in quite a while. I can send my son over in a little bit, after the soup and other food we've gathered have been shared. He can bring back the pot and pick up the box of masks." Sam hesitated before adding, "I'm old enough to remember back when you'd return a dish with something else in it, but these days … well, you know how things are." The haggard man looked like he wanted to cry.

"Yeah, I know," Lucanin said forlornly. "We're all trying to scratch out our own survival. It's hard enough to do that without wearing away what's left of our humanity, too."

The older man heaved a sigh and plastered a smile on his tired face. "Anyway, thanks again for the soup. It'll certainly help, and I'm sure they'll be appreciative of the masks, as well."

As the days passed, Gedney continued making masks as quickly as she could. She never heard anything directly, though little things she was told secondhand indicated people were overjoyed to have them.

When the day came for the couple's ceremony, Gedney showed the bride her mask. The young woman almost broke down in tears in appreciation for the seamstress's thoughtfulness and ingenuity. "It matches so beautifully! To show my gratitude, do you think you'd have time to come to the gathering with the rest of our friends?"

"I can come in briefly to watch the two of you. I'd like to enjoy something pleasant. That's rare enough these days," Gedney responded with a smile that didn't really reach her eyes. "However, I couldn't stay long. The lines of refugees needing food, clothing and masks are increasing all the time. Some have gotten so desperate they walk into our little garden and help themselves, leaving nothing for us or anybody else. Someone has to be there to warn them off!"

Once Gedney finished her latest batch of masks, she needed a break. She left Lucanin in charge of watching the vegetable patch and headed over to the community hall. It had once been a building for religious services and was still used for formal observances like this one. The sturdier buildings had been around since before the attacks. The surviving structures had all been adapted to serve multiple tasks.

Gedney quietly stood in the back of the room and watched the two fresh-faced young people saying their promises to each other. She sighed and got misty-eyed at the optimism of the situation. "May there be peace, warmth and food in the future for all of us," she fervently hoped.

Once the short ceremony was witnessed and completed, Gedney edged toward the rear door to leave the building before the other villagers started filing out. No one in the community had much. If someone had an extra bit of cloth, or some seeds, they gave them to the bride and groom. For most though, all the congregation could do was express their hopes and good wishes to the young couple.

Gedney hesitated. She wanted to enjoy the happy scene. She hadn't even gotten out of the hall before she started feeling a thump in the street. Soon a rumble could be heard as the vibration got closer. Someone in the crowd called, "Oh, no! That's one of those alien all-terrain machines – and it's getting closer!"

That galvanized everyone in the building to go into action. People grabbed whatever they could find if they hadn't thought to tuck a weapon into a pocket or improvised holster.

The machine had found the gathering of people and started shattering the wall of the building to get to them. Everyone massed to attack the vehicle as it eventually broke through the front of the hall. Even an old grandma grabbed her cane and banged on the legs of the advancing alien machine until she was killed. To the old woman's credit, that leg creaked and didn't function smoothly after that.

Momentarily frozen in fear, Gedney finally grabbed a broken piece of two-by-four that had fallen from the shattered wall. She raised it up and struck out at the attacking machine as best she could. Pushing the fragment of wood in between the spaces of the joint on the vehicle's leg, she was able to further cripple it.

With a loud crash and many snaps, the building's compromised wall caved in completely. The collapse ended the screams of the people caught in the center of the meeting hall. After the recent noise and activity, it became deathly quiet. Just the receding impacts from the alien walking vehicle could be felt as it hobbled away from the area.

The entire front half of the hall had been demolished. Gedney looked around and called out, but there was no movement. She tried to search under the rubble. Most of it was too heavy for her to lift. She soon stopped at the grim remains she was able to uncover. It was clear there were no survivors. She was horrified at the carnage she witnessed. As she turned to leave, she found the dusty white mask she'd made for the bride. It was limp and crumpled, stuck in the debris near where the ill-fated couple had last stood. She picked it up in shaking hands. It had one brownish-red splotch of blood on the side, almost in the shape of a teardrop.

Gedney wanted to cry, but she knew she had to move.

That horrible thump-thump reverberated across the village, along with the satisfying creaks from damage caused by the defiant villagers. The machine continued to travel awkwardly down the main road. Another Xanite vehicle had gone around to the outskirts of the village.

She kept moving to stay away from the two machines. Fortunately, the second mechanism continued around the edge of the settlement, so she went unseen. "Almost like it's making sure nobody gets away," she noted through her shock.

With the stained mask still in her hand, she ran back to her little house. Lucanin was nowhere to be found. Not wanting to call out and perhaps draw the attention of the nearby aliens, she went to look around the back garden and surrounding area.

She heard a muffled sound. Her brother was lying on the ground in the middle of the plants, wheezing. Gedney ran up to him. "Luc! What happened?"

"I was out weeding. The alien machines came through. It sounded like they caused some destruction up the way you came. I tried to find out what was happening, but I didn't have time to see much. I never noticed the other one come around behind," he struggled to tell her. "The Xanites came through quickly. They just used one of the articulated arms mounted on their vehicle to hit me as they rushed past. At least they didn't fire on me or I'd be dead. It makes me wonder if they may be saving their ammunition. It could be they're running low, just as we are." He coughed, "Help me stand up."

Gedney eased him inside the modest dwelling. Feeling around his torso, she winced in empathy as he gasped in pain. "It looks like you might have a broken rib or two, but I can get that bandaged up quickly. At least the rest are just bruises and scrapes. I can't help but wonder why they came around in the first place." Gedney talked to him to help keep his focus on something other than the discomfort caused by binding him up.

"They seemed to be heading somewhere fast. I couldn't help but wonder if they're following the refugees," Lucanin speculated aloud.

Thoughtfully, she said, "I don't think so. From the tracks, they went off through our vegetable patch to the rubble beyond. The refugees are all traveling alongside the roads to follow smooth ground as much as possible. Since the aliens' path juts off at an angle to the street, they must be heading somewhere else. Could it mean they're regrouping? Do you think they're going to come back and hit us harder once they've reorganized?"

"I can only hope that isn't so," Lucanin wheezed. The binding around his chest wouldn't let him breathe to speak much.

It was only later that evening that Gedney remembered the unlucky mask she'd carried with her back home. Along with the other newly-made masks, she threw the ill-fated one into the box to be distributed to other survivors. Every refugee took a mask, though the story is told that the person who got the stained mask was killed trying to escape some heavy fighting.

***

"After that, no one wore that covering. Thus, the myth of bad luck following the wedding mask was created," Mr. Jorland said to finish his story.

The youngsters around the campfire roused from the tale. The leader distributed blankets so they'd be warm in the early evening chill.

"Who would want to eat cabbage soup?" one child asked, making a face.

"Weren't you paying attention?" The gray-haired adult said, putting another log on the fire. "That was what they had. Did you pick up on the fact that they shared, even though they didn't have much? Remember that the young woman started making masks to help people and be useful. Using what you have available in creative ways and being an asset to the community are still just as important today."

He was glad to see a bit of enlightenment on the children's faces.

One child had a puzzled look. The leader let the little girl ponder whatever question she was grappling with and gave her time to ask it.

"Why did the Xanites attack us?"

Mr. Jorland scratched his grayed head and pondered the profound question. The children probably wouldn't understand about resources and technological advantages, asymmetric warfare, and things like that. He kept his answer at a basic level for them.

"Well, to put it simply, it's like when you have a problem with another child during a game you're playing together. You both want the same thing. That puts you two at odds at the time, and you may not like each other very much because of that. But eventually, you and the other child come to some agreement about the dispute and then you go back to playing together. Xanites and Humans had a number of disagreements, but we both came to some understandings."

"Oh," the children said collectively, trying to understand what they'd been told.

"I'm glad the attacks ended, but why did they stop?" another child wanted to know.

"There isn't much accurate information from those days, but at one point both sides came together for a ceasefire agreement. The story of the mask maker may have occurred close to that time. That may have been why the alien walkers were leaving in a hurry, though nobody knows," the leader said after a little consideration.

One of the children hastened to ask, "I thought this was just a made-up story. It isn't true, is it?"

"Like I said, there aren't a lot of records from back then. A lot of information was destroyed. By the accounts that did survive, most of the story is correct. Toward the end, some ground vehicles were engaged in what were called 'running battles' against continuing armed resistance and both sides had to fight their way through hostile territory. It could be that the walkers were being chased by a big group of humans putting up resistance. Maybe they didn't want to tangle with them and that's why they didn't stick around."

Another child looked troubled. "Did the girl in the story – Gedney – live to have a happy life? What happened to her?"

The old man looked at the children for a moment. “No one can say. Nobody knows. That snippet of story is all we have of Gedney and her brother Lucanin.”

Jorland looked at all the children, sitting together around the campfire in peace and security. Thoughts of the past came back to him. His mind replayed images that he hadn’t dwelled on in quite a while. He remembered the faces of people he had taught so they would have the means to resist the aggressors. Visions of many of the friends he had worked alongside were evoked, as well.

He was sad, but satisfied that what he had been through had been for such a positive outcome. The land was more fertile and this generation of children would be able to grow more food than their parents had seen. Hopefully, these youngsters would have more opportunities than their grandparents had.

He couldn’t sit and daydream, though. To enjoy the prospects of a better tomorrow, these children had to be told about the past and instructed how to live in the present. With food and security assured, they would be taught the skills that would prepare them for the future. He addressed his charges. “Now, I think that’s enough of the stories. It’s time for you all to head off to your tents. Tomorrow’s a big day.”

The other children got busy and left. Once by himself, one of the quieter boys shyly approached the leader. The lad hadn’t asked questions during the stories as some of the other children had, but this young one obviously had something on his mind.

“My dad has been trying to teach me what he says his dad taught him. He says my grandpa was something called a ‘green braid’ or something. Do you know anything about that?”

The older man turned his attention to the youngster. “I think you might mean ‘Green Beret.’ What was your dad teaching you?”

“He’s been trying to show me things that would toughen me up, as he puts it.”

“Survival training,” the older man said thoughtfully.

“Yes, that’s what Grandpa Saul called it, too.”

"What was your grandfather's full name?" The gray-haired man was curious, now.

"Saul … Saul Johnson. He would have had my dad's last name."

Long forgotten memories flooded the old man's mind. He remembered a Saul Johnson. They had trained together before the decline. They had been two young men in their prime, with cocky smiles and as-yet-unbeaten confidence. They had set out to help save humanity and resurrect civilization. But that was a long time ago. A time early in the invasion, before a lot of deaths, and certainly before old age had set in.

The youngster continued happily, "He likes to talk about something like 'force addition' or something like that, whatever that is."

That made the adult smile. "He's probably talking about something called 'force multiplier.' That was when the Green Berets would work with people who didn't have much. That way they provided people some tools to get things done, and taught them how to accomplish the goals for themselves, even after the Green Berets were gone."

The youngster, with the enthusiasm of youth, looked at the oldster and thought for a minute. "Kind of like what you're doing with us, isn't that right?"

The man smiled a sad smile. *More than you know, kid!* He just nodded at the youth and said, "You listen to what your dad is teaching you. It could come in handy one day. One thing he's doing is teaching perseverance to finish the task at hand. Another thing he's doing is giving you confidence that, no matter what happens, you're up to the challenge."

The child had to think about that statement a moment.

"What I'm trying to show all of you is that there are different ways to solve a problem. If you have any other questions, you can come and ask me. I might even be able to tell you some stories about your grandfather."

Before the boy could ask more questions, the old man called to the children. "Fix your bedrolls and get settled down to sleep. There's a lot to learn tomorrow."

"Good night, Mr. Jorland," they all said, pretty much in unison.

Jorland sighed and reflected on the old friends he'd lost over the years. The sadness of those memories was always lessened by the thoughts of the new friends he'd made along the way, as well. He groaned a little as he used old muscles to get himself up off the log where he'd been resting.

"Maybe these kids will learn an important lesson." He could only hope. Things were slowly getting better, but one wrong move or a single misguided decision could still mean disaster for reemerging civilization.

Jorland went to see that each child was settled in safely. He was gratified to know that the youngsters were growing up with the stories he and others would tell them. Many of the history books were gone. For now, oral tradition was a more practical way of transmitting things like survival, working together as a community and setting and accomplishing goals.

The mutual understanding which led to the ceasefire meant that humans and aliens could begin to trade resources. With time and care, civilization would come back from the brink of chaos and destruction.

Lost knowledge would be found again and earlier abilities would be relearned. That would mean humanity could rebuild their devastated cities. Jorland intended to transmit whatever skills he could, to aid that goal. "And this is how it starts," he said to himself, and gave a weary but satisfied smile.

The Past Creates the Future

The sun peeked through scattered, wispy clouds as a multitude of students scurried around the university campus on their errands or to get to their classes. Colleges staunchly tried to uphold many of the traditions and standards from the "before times," so Zac Johnson was considered a graduate student. He approached the squat history building to meet with his professor.

People weren't comfortable with tall buildings. Superstitions abounded surrounding the few remaining skeletons of old-technology skyscrapers. Those derelicts were testaments to the Xanite destruction. They also stood as a reminder of lost abilities and knowledge.

Current engineers couldn't yet copy preinvasion elevators, though they were working on it. The need for staircases also forced buildings to be built lower. The young grad student stood and marveled at the height. He was impressed that this structure was three stories. With youthful energy, he quickly ascended the steps to go inside.

Young Zac had shaggy blond hair. People didn't get very frequent haircuts, since only the well-to-do could afford someone with the expertise and equipment. He certainly couldn't. He only cared about finishing his studies. "I know my professor has been getting a little upset with me concerning my graduate thesis, but I only recently found something that might fit."

History professor Janella Dodson was awaiting the young man's arrival with mounting frustration. She found his indecision over a dissertation topic worrying. Janella's specialty was historical records of the collapse period, so she had been trying to steer her uncertain student in that direction.

A shaft of sunlight coming through the window at her back highlighted the professor's silver-white hair. She checked her ancient watch yet again. It was a precious relic from before the decline of society.

She looked up just as the young man bustled energetically through her office door. The woman pushed her glasses, another useful artifact, up on her nose. She motioned to a chair in front of her desk for him to sit. She gave her attention to her visitor and allowed him a few minutes to collect himself. He was grateful for the chance to catch his breath from rushing up the three flights of stairs.

"Do you have any news to tell me concerning a topic for your thesis?" She hoped he'd resolve his indecisiveness soon. She had other students to deal with, as well.

"I have some ideas," he said sheepishly. "Right now, I'm thinking of something like 'invasion-era people, artifacts and beliefs.' One commonly held superstition during the period was that people wore masks to hide ugly faces or disfigurements caused by disease or war. Older people have told about the various traditions and legends of that time. I want to incorporate some of that. I'll talk to family members for any information and family documents pertaining to that time."

At last, the professor saw a glimmer of enthusiasm in her student! "That sounds good, but remember," she held up her finger to admonish her student.

Zac knew where she was going and said with her, "Try to broaden the search and dig deeper to confirm your thesis' premise. And always verify your information."

The young man smiled with enthusiasm to show he understood. "I remember what you've taught. So far, I'm having trouble locating enough records to start putting together much information, but I'm working on it."

Janella understood the lack of collapse-era documents. "Beginning locally with family and neighbors is just a start. Oral history is a good foundation, but your search must be expanded from there. The regional archives will help, once you know what geographic area will be of interest."

"I intend to do that. Correlating whatever documents I can find with oral history from the decline will further our knowledge of what transpired in that timeframe."

The professor nodded appreciatively. "That sounds good. Get to it, then. You don't have a lot of time." She smiled at his youthful energy as he quickly left her office.

He exited the building with renewed direction. "At a family gathering, I recall overhearing a story that a family member of ours had done some interesting stuff during the invasion and subsequent collapse. That would be something I'd like to investigate. This research will satisfy what I need to do for the degree and it'll fill a personal desire to dig into family history."

Zac traveled back to visit his hometown that weekend on a regularly scheduled horse-drawn wagon. Few combustion engines were still in use. He passed the sign denoting the extent of university property. About six hours later, the tired horses continued beyond the signpost of the village where his family still lived. Most of the sign was shot out, but some letters could be read: "cinnati." Everyone still knew it as Cincinnati, though.

Once home, he talked to his mother, who told him she didn't know of anyone interesting on her side of their family tree. "Why don't you talk to your father?" she encouraged him.

That evening, after greeting his father and discussing how his studies were going, Zac asked, "I understand we have at least one family member who played an important role during the collapse. Do you know anything about him or who I might ask to get information on him?"

His father thought about it. "There is my brother. He'd be your Uncle Samuel. He's older than I am. I was way too young to remember our grandfather, Saul, but Sam told a few stories involving granddad back when we were younger. He may still remember a few of them."

The next day, after another uncomfortable wagon ride, Zac was knocking on the door of his uncle's place.

"Hi, Uncle Samuel! Do you remember any stories about Great-Grandpa Saul? I vaguely recall hearing a few at family gatherings." The young man excitedly asked, with more enthusiasm than patience.

Samuel scratched the gray stubble that was always on his cheeks. "Come in, Zac! Sit down, and I'll try to remember some of the stories for you. I'll bet your dad sent you. I recall telling him stories about Grandpa Saul. I remember Grandpa told me many times that it was important to remember and pass on this knowledge. Taking a wagon has become too hard for my old bones, and it takes too much time to travel. I couldn't come to you, but now that you're here it's time to share these things with you."

The old man stood in thought for a moment. He suddenly smiled. "I know. Grandpa Saul's things are probably in the attic!"

After briefly searching and loudly sneezing from all the dust the mementos had accumulated, the old man brought his treasures back. Zac sat on the couch with his uncle while the elderly man reverently wiped some remaining grime from the covers of the boxes he had brought down to show his nephew.

In one box was a collection of old, yellowed photos of people in strange, mottled garb. They stood there in relaxed poses and showed confident grins. The men in the pictures held what Zac recognized as weapons, so he surmised that this may have been just before a lot of the fighting that had occurred during the invasion. There were other pictures of the men, obviously in more posed shots, wearing strange hats.

With a wrinkled hand, Samuel picked up one picture of a young man with blond hair and eyes much like Zac's. "This is your great-grandfather."

Zac studied the young man with the grin so similar to his own. He reached back into the box and looked at some of the other pictures. "He's in this one as well. But who is this dark-haired man with him? They obviously were friends."

Samuel reached for the photo of the two men and turned it over. "This says 'Saul and Jason.' I'll have to try to remember if he mentioned a Jason in his stories." The old man reached into the box for a group photo of a bunch of men in those same green hats. Underneath the photo were the names of the men in the picture. "Here's a Jason Jorland." In examining the picture closer, he decided, "It looks like it would be the same guy."

The old man's eyes went unfocused for a bit. When he refocused on Zac, he said, "I seem to recall my dad telling me about a camping trip with an adult leader who was teaching all the kids how to survive. That was more necessary back then, you know. His name was also Jorland. I wonder if it could have been the same person."

As the memory became clearer in his mind, the old man went on. "My dad used to talk about how your Great-Grandpa Saul would also try to teach him things like surviving off the land. Dad used to laugh and tell the story how he used to call the group 'green braids' till Jorland told him it was Green Berets."

"Is that what they're wearing in the pictures?" As his uncle talked, Zac reached for the second box, which had other remnants of the past in it.

"That's right." The old man pulled out a hat like the men in the pictures wore. "This, my boy, is a green beret. From the stories my dad told, it was something very prized by Grandpa Saul and others like him."

Zac was amazed by what he was hearing. As he put the hat back in the box, he said, "I knew some of my family members lived through the invasion, but I didn't know any were this important."

The two looked into the second box and found a piece of stiff fabric like the men in the pictures had been wearing on the sleeves of their uniforms. Samuel pointed a shaky finger at the object. "My dad told me Grandpa Saul called that a 'patch.' He explained to me that this one is a depiction of machine cogs. In this patch, you see that one cog meshes with another.

I remember him saying that cogs were what made a machine go."

The older man reminisced. "It designated the group he was with. They were sent out to defend people and help teach them how to fight and handle things for themselves. I remember being shown a car engine. Much like that engine, they were the parts that would get society going again."

Zac looked closely at the keepsake. "I notice that around these cogs are the words, 'Continuity of Government and Society.' I can't help but see that the first letters of the words spell out c-o-g-s."

"Yes, I recall your great-grandfather saying the government loved its … oh, what was the word?" The older man had to stop and think. "Acronyms! That's the word! The government loved its acronyms! They would always put shorter names to take the place of saying a whole bunch of words."

"I'll add 'cogs,' to my search as well as Jason Jorland and Saul. I can work out from there." The younger man set the items down to write notes so he wouldn't forget. "Do the pictures say where they were taken?"

"Look through and see. You're welcome to take whatever helps you in your search," the older man said.

"This place in the picture seems very utilitarian, which would probably make it military. It's also interesting to see something in such good shape. Do you remember any military places somewhere around here?"

Scratching his whiskers, the old man replied, "Not that I recall. However, travel is slow, so most people don't seem to journey very far from where they're born. It may be further out than most people venture. I recall my dad retelling stories he heard about people traveling all around the world. I always wondered if that was made up! This place in the picture, wherever it is, may have long since been abandoned or destroyed."

"If he was fairly close by, the local library might have some information. I'll check there and see what I can find. This research might take a little while. Since it took most of a day to get here, would you mind if I stayed overnight at some point?" At his uncle's agreement, he said, "Thanks, Uncle Samuel!"

With enthusiasm, the young man started to hurry off then turned back to his uncle. "I'll give these pictures back once I'm done." He carefully put the pictures of the two Green Beret soldiers in a safe pocket.

Another painful wagon ride later, Zac was beginning his research at the nearest library.

"We have some pre-collapse books that survived the turmoil, but most of the records that were in other forms didn't seem to fare well with the pulses we got in the area," the older man behind the desk told him.

"Can you show me anything on those 'pulses' as you called them?" Zac knew he needed to start somewhere, and that seemed a good point to begin.

"Right this way," the man said, leading him to a dusty area of the library filled with little-used technical manuals. The man handed Zac a few books and pointed to more on the shelves if he wanted to look further into the subject.

"Well, let's see here. So, 'pulses' refer to some electromagnetic waves that disrupt electronic machinery. Many military installations were hit with these pulses as well as lasers. Makes sense that the information stored on those devices wouldn't survive. I imagine pulses would be like dousing a book with water." The eager student scanned through volumes and journals, gaining an insight into some of the happenings that people had lived through during the early days of the collapse.

"Here's something interesting; back then they had these things called 'data storage devices' that were pretty small. Some were no bigger than my thumbnail! It's no wonder many got crushed or lost during the upheaval. Some were locked. 'Encrypted' is the word these books used. To this day, they can't be opened. Now, there are few machines that can actually read them if they aren't locked. It's amazing how much they depended on these things. I begin to understand why society came to a standstill – nothing worked and information was immediately lost."

The librarian left to continue his duties, smiling at the young man's enthusiasm.

Eventually, Zac's desire to know more warred with his bleary eyes. He was interrupted as the librarian came to tell him that it was almost time to close. With much more information yet to be found, he knew he'd have to return again for further research. "Can you tell me if there were any military buildings nearby?"

"There are none that I know of. However, the previous librarian is still in town. Since she's been here longer, she might remember something from before my time."

"How can I find her?"

"It's a short walk down this lane in front of the library. When you get to the end of it, turn left. It's the little place with the big cabbage patch in front. She's old-fashioned that way. A lot of older people are still afraid of starvation."

"I've read they went through lean times back then," Zac nodded in understanding.

Zac gathered his notes and left the library, walking down the lane till it came to an end. He knew that trying to make it back to his uncle's place that night, and back again the next day would take too much time. He noted a little rooming house where he could stay overnight. Walking on, he found the house with the prodigious vegetable garden.

His knock was met by an old woman with faded blue eyes. "Hello, young man," she said in a kind and quiet voice. "What brings you here this evening?"

"Hello. I was at the library doing research and the man there mentioned I might talk to you. If I may, I'd like to ask you a few questions. I'm trying to find information on a relative who lived during the collapse. So far I haven't been able to find anything specific. He probably would have been somewhere around this general area. Can you give me some insight where I might look? I also wonder if you could tell me if there was some sort of military center nearby."

The old woman's face creased in a wrinkled smile. "I'm glad to see people using the remaining resources to do research and relearn the old knowledge, young man. If your relative lived in this region, you might go to the archives building. It's located way out of town, but there will be a regular wagon going to the area tomorrow. You're in luck; any military information will be located in the same area as the archive center. Everything was consolidated in the old military buildings since they were sturdy."

Zac thanked the old woman and walked back to the rooming house. There he got a room for the night and, in the morning, caught the wagon to the archive center. Once there, he listened to someone explain what he and a few other intrepid people were seeing.

"The building is made out of something called reinforced concrete, so it survived the poundings that destroyed many civilian buildings. That's why all the archive papers are stored here. If you'll follow me, you will see a few of the remaining computers in the region. They were protected from the electromagnetic pulses and actually still work. We're very proud of them!"

The group walked inside, passing from a warm early summer morning into a cool expanse. Zac couldn't help but run his hand over the sturdy structure as he passed inside. "Concrete," he pondered. There were a few areas where it had been chipped and he saw small rocks and a rusted metal rod embedded into the material. As his eyes adjusted to the darker interior, he paid attention to the guide's explanations.

"We have power collectors that can run the lights and equipment in this area for a few hours a day. As you can see, we have people who are doing research using some of these machines."

Zac spoke up, "I have some research to do, on two people who lived through the collapse. I have a picture of my great-grandfather and a friend of his. Could you help me find more information about them and the buildings in the picture? Do you think that would be possible?"

"Yes, young man, we have enough assistants to help each of you, if you want it."

At the guide's gesture, a young woman approached them and introduced herself. "I'm Darla. I'm an apprentice here. Do you need help?"

Zac spent a speechless moment looking at the pretty girl. The guide left, a little bemused at Zac's reaction.

The young man soon roused himself from his tongue-tied state. "Can you help me find out anything about this picture and the people in it?"

After pondering the picture, the pretty girl walked Zac over to an empty computer station. "The building behind them might just be on this base. Let's see…" She fiddled with the keys and brought up some old pictures of the area.

"Yes, that could be the old armory on the base here," she said. "If they were here, they might have information accessible in this building. Can you give me their names?"

He stuttered and finally came up with the men's names.

"Jorland and Johnson. I'll go see what I can find and be back as soon as I can. If you stay here, the computer won't be grabbed by anybody else till we can finish." Darla walked purposefully to a storage area. She was completely unaware that Zac sat there ogling her till she disappeared around a corner.

The young woman soon came back with something in her hand. "This is all I could find quickly." She put it into a receptacle in the computer. Zac recognized it as one of those data storage devices he'd read about.

She pressed play and the screen lit up with the face of the dark-haired man Zac recognized as Jason Jorland. The man in the video began to speak.

"Jorland here. This is report number 24 of our ongoing efforts to support the resistance movement in this area. As you can see, we've been successful in finding whatever food was available. A couple of the civilians and I went out and scouted some of the abandoned stores. We loaded up with food and medical supplies and brought them here. The food went to the cooking area you can see over there. This is really more of a soup kitchen because that will feed the most people. At least they're getting fed."

The camera kept running as Jason stood there for a moment. He was tired, dirty, and at a loss for words. It was clear that he was doing his best in a difficult and trying situation. "Saul, why don't you come around and talk about what you've been working on?"

The camera angle was jostled, showing an overcast sky and smoke in the area. Zac surmised that they had probably been under attack recently. The camera steadied and a familiar blond-haired man addressed them.

"If you'd pan over there, Headquarters can see that, with the medicine we found, we now have a functioning triage center. We scrounged what vials, pills and syringes we could from nearby pharmacies before looters took what was left. It may not be a hospital, but it can take care of basic medical needs, and that's more than the people here had before. Slowly, as we provide the things like medicine and food, we're beginning to draw in people needing assistance from outlying areas, too. We give these people information and direction. In turn, they add to the skills we need, and with more able-bodied people, we're able to put up a bigger resistance."

Both Saul and Jason had soot-covered faces and looked haggard. Their clothes hung loosely on their bodies.

Saul continued his report. "The people have to take things like sheets, rip them up into bandages and boil them for use. It's the best they can do, but it's a start. Now, we're looking to find people with any kind of medical knowledge."

He talked as he walked along to another building. "Here Jason and I have recruited some area mechanics to repair whatever they can. Most had their own tools, but we were able to scrounge some more from stores and shops. As you can see, they are concentrating on cars, but they are also repairing whatever pickup trucks and semis they can find that might still be usable. The rest that aren't repairable will be used to create a barrier around this encampment that will protect the people inside from ground assault. We're still working on how to protect them from potential aerial poundings."

Jason spoke out from behind the camera, "We both have suggested to the various people, whether cooks, medics or mechanics, to take on apprentices to pass on knowledge. At this point, books are not too practical for people who might have to flee at a moment's notice. Electronics aren't always available or usable, but we are working with another group to try to establish an informational materials repository in a common, easily defended location. We've chosen the Wright-Patterson area as a perfect place for data storage."

The camera was still on Saul, who made a derisive face at Jason's use of words. "Yes, it's called a library. We've also rounded up a few librarians to staff the place. We found the Wright State Library. Some of the contents survived and are being moved as we speak." He nodded and ended the report with, "We've done a lot so far to stabilize the situation in this area, but we've got plans to do more. That's about all that can be said at this point. Progress continues – Jorland and Johnson out!"

***

Zac sat back in his chair, wondering at what he'd just viewed. It was staggering to watch and listen to the two men in their prime. He turned to Darla and gave her an appreciative smile. "That was amazing! Can we find any more about them?"

Smiling, the young librarian had Zac wait while she returned the data storage device to where it belonged. It took a while, but she was able to find something else. When it was played, Zac again saw the two intrepid soldiers. In the background, he heard explosions.

***

"Jorland and Johnson here," the voice said, but the camera was being jostled because the two were running, along with many others. "We don't have enough ammunition to hold out long, but a couple of the hunters have brought out crossbows. I have to take a look at the walkers that are attacking us. I think that they have optics that a bolt could probably disable, if these guys are accurate enough. I'm going to talk to the hunters now…"

There was more jostling and then the record faded. When it began again, Jorland was talking to some pretty grimy guys.

"Do you think you can hit that optical input from this far out?" Jorland pointed to a schematic he had drawn to show them where they should aim their bolts to blind the machines.

"We might be able to do it, but we'd have a better chance if we let them get a bit closer. That's a pretty small target to hit accurately this far out," one of the hunters said. The others nodded in agreement.

The record faded and resumed with Saul. "That worked pretty slick – disabled the optics so they couldn't see. Unfortunately, the walkers kept advancing in their original direction and one of them is about to break through our makeshift barrier."

A woman stood next to Saul with a bow in hand. What she brought up to nock was more of a pointed stick than a slim, manufactured arrow. In the video, she got closer and expertly shot the makeshift projectile into the joint area of one of the machines. It hung there for a while, but was soon crunched by the action of the hinge. However, the hardwood stick damaged the hinge just enough to cripple the movement in that leg. She looked for an opportunity to get close and disable the other leg to further immobilize the oncoming walker. In the background, others were attempting to do the same.

***

Zac observed the look his great-grandfather gave to the woman. The young man noticed that she was pretty, even though she was dirty and her clothes were scruffy. He understood the loving glance. From some of the old pictures that had survived, he surmised this was probably his great-grandmother when she was much younger. The youthful student hadn't realized that he came from such intrepid people.

The camera turned and showed a walker. A tall, skinny figure emerged. The creature wore dark, bulky armor. A voice Zac recognized as Jason's directed the people to concentrate on the nearer walker as they repelled the aliens. The fleeing Xanite hesitated, looking back for a moment to see if it was being followed. Then it frantically continued, awkwardly trying to run across the ice and escape.

***

The video focused on Saul again. He gestured to a fallen alien machine. "This proves the optics are vulnerable and the hinges can be targeted to disable their walkers. One machine has backed off, but the other refused to disengage from fighting, despite being blinded, and kept coming through our barrier. This shows that the alien armored vehicles can be defeated. This is a good way to incapacitate them. Also, we've found their gauss weapons don't appear to be much more advanced than our own. However, not all of their walkers seem to be equipped with them."

He looked at the camera. "These are important points of information. Their tech level seems to be only slightly above ours when it comes to weapons. So far, we've fought back and won. With more organization, we could drive the Xanites out of this area completely. Command, if you're getting this, let others know of the vulnerabilities we've discussed. We could sure use knowledge of additional weaknesses that others have found."

Saul looked hesitant. "I don't know if you're still out there and receiving these." He stopped, as if hoping for a response – a response that probably never came. "That's all for now. Out."

***

The last record showed Saul and the same woman they had seen earlier. This time, they were both older and had kids. Also in the video were Jason and a woman Zac didn't recognize. Zac commented, "It's strange to see all these people, first when they were so young, and then as they got older."

He asked Darla, "Where would that last video be located? Can you tell?"

She stepped away to do some research. When she came back she answered, "I was able to find it was in a place called Dayton."

"I guess I need to travel there next. I don't suppose you'd care to accompany me?" he hopefully asked the pretty librarian.

Darla shook her head to say no, but gave a sad smile. "There are others to help with research." She turned reluctantly to go, but asked the cute guy, "Do you think you might be back here some other time?"

"I'm sure I'll have more research to do later. Maybe I can see you again, if that would be all right. I could ask for you specifically, Darla!"

Another painfully long wagon ride took him back to the little library where he had started his research, and he found another scheduled wagon to Dayton. The town was much smaller than in the past – only a little bigger than a village due to the destruction of much of the surrounding area. His tired rear end could take no more, so he found a place for the night. He asked the innkeeper and his wife if they knew of any relatives of Jason Jorland. They shook their heads no. He had missed the inn's evening meal offering, so he went to a nearby pub for something to eat and to ask questions of the people there.

"Do you know of any relatives of this man?" Zac asked the bartender. The man looked thoughtfully at the picture. He pointedly looked at the empty space in front of Zac, indicating that he should buy a drink to get an answer. Once the drink was set in front of the young man, the bartender opened up.

"I can't really tell. He looks a little familiar, but that picture is old. There might be a family resemblance to a friend of a staff member. She comes around every once in a while. You might talk to the waitress over there." The bartender pointed at a woman serving a nearby table and turned away, busying himself with the other customers.

Zac motioned for the woman to come over. She had noticed his attention. "Actually, Zima serves this area," she told him brusquely.

"I just want to talk to you," Zac said.

"Whatever you're wanting, I'm not that kind of girl," she said in a huff.

"No, I would just like to talk about these two guys," he said, and showed her the picture of Johnson and Jorland.

She stopped and looked at it. "I don't know who the blond guy is, but the dark-haired guy has a resemblance to my roommate, Jasonia."

"I would just like to see if she recognizes this man, honest." Zac looked as sincere as he could, and added, "Could you help me? Please?"

"I suppose I could let you follow me home. It's nearby. Just don't expect to be invited in," she added. At Zac's thanks, she hurried off to tend to her own section.

Zac ate his dinner and waited for the woman to get off work. Once she motioned to him to follow her, he introduced himself. "I'm Zac, by the way. And you are?" He waited for an awkward few minutes before she responded.

"I'm Tanyelle. Nice to meet you, Zac." They walked along in uncomfortable silence. "Here we are," she finally said.

Zac walked up the path to her front door, but stayed back respectfully when she went to open it.

"Hey, Jasonia, are you here? Some guy outside would like a word with you."

"Since when do you call me Jasonia instead of Jay?" A woman with Jason's dark hair and brown eyes stepped up to the doorway. "Is this the guy? He's kind of cute."

Zac hesitated, not knowing what he might be getting himself into, but bravely stepped closer to their porch. "I would just like to talk to you. I'm doing research on the two guys in this picture. I have to admit, you do resemble Jason, the dark-haired guy. Do you have a Jason in your family line?"

The dark-haired woman was silent for a little bit, surprise showing on her face. "Would you know what this man's last name is?"

"I've learned his name is Jason Jorland, if that helps. And the other guy is Saul Johnson. He's my great-grandfather. They were friends."

She looked at the young man in astonishment for a few moments. "They were more than just friends. They were what my great-granddad called 'battle buddies.' Why don't you come in and we'll talk about it."

Inside, Jasonia went to find some mementoes of her great-grandfather. Zac told her of the patch he'd seen and the green berets they'd worn.

Jasonia brought out some papers written by Jason. In them, he told of the deprivation of those harsh winter months. He wrote of his grief at losing the love of his life. He and Valerie had a child, though, and that helped him through his loss. Eventually he had grandchildren, which was how Jasonia came to be born.

"We wanted to remember his hard work and sacrifice. My parents had expected a boy. They had to alter great-granddad's name slightly to fit a girl. I recall he would teach the kids about survival. I do that today, although things aren't as dire as they used to be." She reached for Zac's picture to look at it again. "You look like him – Saul, was it?"

Zac nodded, while writing down notes about Jason. Zac listened while Jasonia read from her great-grandfather's diary. The young researcher was surprised to learn that Jason had saved some people who were fleeing from the attacking

Xanites. In one passage, Jason recounted a time when the town was attacked by walkers. Many refugees survived because of the two soldiers' quick action, but Jason was hurt helping them to escape the resulting fires.

He gave credit to his friend Saul's assistance, writing that his friend was crucial in saving the people of the town, as well. The survivors worked together with the two soldiers in successfully fighting off the Xanites. Afterward, Jason was able to receive medical assistance, which was hard to find back then. It took a while, but he did recover from his wounds. He credited Valerie for that.

"Perhaps that was where he first met Valerie and eventually they had a child together," Zac surmised.

Jasonia nodded. "He detailed his misgivings about his ability to continue the important mission he had been given. He came to the realization that, even though he couldn't possibly rebuild the entire country, he could teach the family and friends around him about the things he remembered from his past. That way, he was actually passing on knowledge and aiding the rebirth of society. His teachings helped, in some way, to get us where we are today."

***

Zac returned home with interesting information about Saul and his friend. Zac was inspired by their determination in the face of such odds. He was more confident when he had to give his dissertation. "It's not as life threatening as what those two soldiers had experienced."

Standing in front of the professors, he smiled at his girlfriend, Darla, as he concluded his speech:

"These people were supposed to 'make government and society go,' much like the cogs depicted on their patches. However, these men weren't machines themselves. They suffered hunger and wounds along with the refugees, and had self-doubts and misgivings about being able to fulfill the great task they were given."

Zachary exhaled. "It has been a few generations since the Xanite invasion, and we're still getting things back together. The peace treaty we signed with them has allowed stability. The old books have rekindled lost knowledge. While we haven't recovered the totality of the preinvasion level of technical expertise yet, we are advancing."

He looked up to address the audience. "We know now that we aren't alone in the universe. That has changed the way we view ourselves. It has altered the way we treat each other. It has made us more mindful of the way we use our planet's resources. It has modified the way we view society and the individual's role in the social order. Sharing and contributing to the greater good are looked on with more importance than ever before."

"With a better future comes the responsibility to learn from the past – both the bright points of bravery and perseverance, and the dark times of despair and surrender. As bleak as those times were, we should strive to remember that many people laid the foundation for what we have today. We have an obligation to move forward. We owe them all a great debt, and we must be mindful of their sacrifices. Let us try to emulate the courage and dedication of those who chose to rebuild society instead of living off of the suffering of others. We must see to it that their deeds are never forgotten, even if we never learn their names."

Sometime after his dissertation, Zac gave the pictures back so Uncle Samuel could cherish and preserve them. "If you want to pass them on, I'd like to have them someday," he said with sincerity.

Zac continued in his quest to find more information. Through the years, his searches found very few remaining documents on other Green Berets. However, he learned from surviving records that many of them had been sent out to help across the nation. He decided to take on the task of finding all the details he could about the preinvasion era and the contributions of the unsung heroes during the invasion. He considered it a sacred duty to pass on that knowledge to others. In that way he would continue their rebuilding process.

***

The older man sat in the new office building on the campus, the sun through the window giving his white hair a yellow glow. The structure was amazing, towering at six stories, and his aging joints were glad for the addition of elevators. The old scholar was also heartened that his searches for more documents from the invasion era were now being taken up by his assistants. It wasn't lost on him that his professor had kindled that spark in him, and he was doing the same for another generation.

He looked at the picture displayed on his impressive desk – it was the photograph given to him by his uncle of the two cocky young soldiers who took on a daunting task. He contemplated a fitting end to a research paper he would soon publish.

"Our living memory of the Xanite invasion is beginning to fade. A younger generation has come to power in a world that is changing very fast. Our understanding of the upheaval may not fully come into focus due to insufficient records. During my years leading some historical research into the era, I have chronicled the lives of some of the participants. This is my best attempt to fill out the timeline."

The elderly man nodded in agreement as he silently read on. "My research is mainly built around in-person interviews, videos and surviving government documents concerning two specific Green Berets. A few diaries where the exploits of these almost mythic figures were mentioned certainly kept me fascinated in my explorations."

Memories of the videos he had watched played in his mind. He sighed in equal amounts of satisfaction and regret. "What they accomplished is typical of what others across the country did, with no recognition or outside help. They truly lifted us up out of the darkness. This work is to provide information to future scholars, and perhaps spark inquiry into other unknown heroes."

The old professor sighed. "And that is how it started." He signed his paper, "Zachary Johnson, Professor of History, Wright State University."

About the Author

Anne K. Nagel avoids labels, but being retired is one she doesn't mind. She lives in Anchorage, Alaska. Writing is Anne's creative outlet, allowing her the opportunity to explore new worlds of romance and adventure. Anne enjoys stories with happy endings.

www.ingramcontent.com/pod-product-compliance
Lightning Source LLC
Chambersburg PA
CBHW070626130626
46555CB00006B/2461

* 9 7 8 0 9 8 8 9 6 7 6 5 6 *